Until the War Took You

The Story of Clara and James

by Demontray Quintez Grigsby

Until the War Took You

The Story of Clara and James

© 2025 Demontray Quintez Grigsby

All rights reserved. No part of this book may be reproduced, stored, or transmitted in any form or by any means without the prior written permission of the author.

This is a work of fiction. Names, characters, places, and events are either products of the author's imagination or used fictitiously.

Printed in the United States of America

Table of Contents

Chapter One: Maury Roots 1

Chapter Two: Summer of Us 15

Chapter Three: A Soldier's Oath 30

Chapter Four: Ink-Stained Promises 45

Chapter Five: Her Call to Serve 60

Chapter Six: Training Grounds 77

Chapter Seven: Chasing Shadows 94

Chapter Eight: A Reunion in Italy 113

Chapter Nine: The Return to Battle 129

Chapter Ten: Omaha Beach 142

Chapter Eleven: The Telegram 159

Chapter Twelve: His Letters, Her Legacy 173

Chapter Thirteen: The Return Home 186

Dedication

For every heart that held on through war, and every letter that never stopped believing.

About the Author

Demontray Quintez Grigsby is a Southern storyteller with a passion for tales of love, resilience, and history. A student of both political science and human nature, his writing blends the poetic rhythm of the past with emotionally rich characters. Until the War Took You is his tribute to those whose love endured distance, hardship, and sacrifice.

Introduction

Until the War Took You is more than a story of love—it is a tribute to the endurance of hope during one of the darkest chapters in history. Set against the backdrop of World War II, this novel follows Clara Evans and James Whitaker, two childhood friends from Columbia, Tennessee, whose bond is tested by distance, duty, and the unimaginable weight of war. Their story unfolds through letters, memories, and moments that capture both the heartbreak and the courage of those who waited—and those who fought to return.

This book was written to honor not only the soldiers who served, but also the women who waited, who worked, who changed the world from the home front and beyond. It speaks to the sacrifices made in silence, the love kept alive through ink and devotion, and the healing found through service, sacrifice, and strength.

Clara and James's journey is fiction, but their emotions are not. They belong to every generation that has loved across oceans, that has believed in reunion despite the odds. This is for them. This is for you.

Chapter One: Maury Roots

They had always lived next door to each other.

On the quiet stretch of Maple Street in Columbia, Tennessee—just past the old feed store and across from the First Baptist Church—James Whitaker and Clara Evans grew up like siblings, though even in childhood, there was a difference in the way they watched one another. Their houses sat side by side, divided by a narrow white fence that leaned slightly from years of climbing, sitting, and passing notes between slats.

Clara's house smelled of cinnamon and garden soil. Her mother kept a line of potted violets on the windowsill and always had something baking in the oven. James's home was louder—filled with brothers, muddy boots, and the scent of tobacco from his father's pipe. Clara, an only child, often snuck over to the Whitakers' back porch just to sit in the noise, to be part of the commotion.

James was always in motion. If he wasn't fishing off the edge of the Duck River, he was racing his brothers through the cornfields or hammering together lopsided tree forts. Clara followed him like a shadow—bandaging his scrapes, helping him put frogs in mason jars, and learning early on that quiet could be its own kind of strength.

By the time they were ten, they had a routine. Saturdays meant long bike rides to the general store for penny candy. Sundays, they sat together in church, fidgeting in the pews until Mrs. Whitaker shot them a look sharp enough to freeze their giggles. Summers were their favorite. They'd swim in Marrowbone Lake, barefoot and sunburned, sharing secrets while they watched the clouds drift above the hills.

Their friendship was the kind that made other kids jealous. They moved through the world as a unit—James with his quick grin and dirt-streaked cheeks, Clara with her sketchbook and sunhat, always just a half-step behind him.

No one thought much of it at first. In Maury, everyone's lives overlapped. But as they grew older, people began to whisper.

"Those two are thick as thieves," Mrs. Holcomb said to the grocer one day, watching the pair walk past. "Wouldn't surprise me one bit if they ended up married."

At the time, Clara rolled her eyes and tossed a peach pit toward the fence. "People in this town have too much time and not enough sense," she muttered.

James grinned. "Guess we better start charging admission."

They laughed, but the seed had been planted. After that, every touch lingered a little longer. Every glance became a question neither of them dared answer.

By their sophomore year at Central High, the shape of their world had begun to change.

The country was still clawing its way out of the Great Depression, and whispers of war in Europe had begun to creep into their small-town newspaper. But in Columbia, life continued at its usual, unhurried pace. Boys helped their fathers on the farms, girls helped their mothers sew dresses or tend shop counters, and every Friday night, the whole town gathered in the school gymnasium to cheer on the Lions.

James had started working afternoons at the Evans Hardware store, stocking shelves and unloading deliveries. He'd grown into his frame by then—tall and lean with calloused hands and shoulders shaped by farm chores. Clara noticed the change more than she let on. He had the same eyes, the same smile that crinkled at the corners, but there was something new in the way he walked, something quieter and more assured.

Clara spent most afternoons at the library or sketching by the river, where the sounds of the world faded behind the rustle of leaves and the low murmur of the water. She had an eye for capturing life as it passed—Mrs. Gilmore at her sewing machine, Mr. Crawford's bent frame over the shoe repair bench, even the Whitaker boys playing marbles on the sidewalk. But her favorite subject, the one she never quite managed to draw the way she saw him, was James.

They still spent their evenings on Clara's front porch swing, talking about everything and nothing. Homework, plans for after graduation, whether or not the Yankees had a chance that year. James would carve little notches into the armrest with his pocketknife while Clara read aloud from whatever book she was working through.

Sometimes, they sat in silence, listening to the cicadas hum in the trees and the gentle creak of the swing as it moved back and forth. That silence, full of all things they didn't yet have the words to say, become its own kind of language.

"I was thinking about enlisting," James said one evening in late October. His voice was casual, but Clara heard the weight beneath it.

She lowered her book, heart suddenly thudding in her chest. "You're seventeen."

"Eighteen in four months. The recruiter comes through Columbia twice a year. He said I could sign early if I had permission."

Clara stared at the porch boards, unsure of what to say. The war felt far away, like something happening in black-and-white pictures across the ocean. But now it was in her backyard, sitting beside her, speaking in James's voice.

"Why?" she asked finally.

James was quiet for a long time. "I don't know. Maybe because my dad did. Maybe because it feels like the world's changing and I don't want to sit here and do nothing."

Clara swallowed hard. "You'd leave all this?"

He gave a small smile. "Not all of it. Just… for a while."

That night, when he walked her to the door, she didn't let go of his hand right away. They stood under the porch light, caught in the strange gravity that had begun to pull them together more and more lately.

"Just promise me," Clara said softly, "that if you go… you'll come back."

James nodded, pressing her hand to his chest. "You'll be the reason I do."

By spring of senior year, there was no more pretending.

Everyone saw it. Teachers. Neighbors. Even Clara's mother, who had once chuckled when Clara insisted she and James were just friends, now looked at her daughter with quiet understanding. "Love doesn't always arrive with a grand entrance," she'd said one evening while hemming Clara's graduation dress. "Sometimes it just grows, slow and steady, until it's the only thing you recognize."

Clara wasn't sure exactly when she'd fallen in love with James Whitaker. Maybe it was the summer he stayed up all night fixing her father's broken fence. Maybe it was when he stood up to a boy who teased her about her lisp in seventh grade. Or maybe it was every day since childhood, stacked one on top of the other like letters in a drawer, waiting to be read.

Whatever the moment, she felt it now with every glance, every shared laugh, every brush of his hand against hers.

Their first kiss came on a soft April night.

They'd walked down to the river after dusk, the air heavy with magnolia and the scent of fresh rain. Fireflies blinked in and out of the shadows like tiny stars, and the moonlight painted the surface of the water in silver.

Clara stood on the edge of the bank, her bare toes dipping into the cool current, arms wrapped around herself. James came up behind her, close but not too close, like he always did—giving her space, but never too much.

"You ever wonder what it would've been like," he asked, "if we'd been born in a different time?"

Clara tilted her head. "What do you mean?"

"I don't know… Somewhere without war hanging over us. Where the biggest thing we had to worry about was which church picnic to go to."

She gave a soft laugh, but it faded quickly. "Yeah. I think about it a lot."

James reached for her hand. When their fingers touched, it was as if the air shifted—no longer spring, no longer war or peace—just the stillness between two hearts finally brave enough to meet halfway.

"I don't want to leave without knowing what this is," he said. "Not just thinking about it. Not just guessing."

Clara turned to face him. "Then stop guessing."

And she kissed him.

It was tender, a little unsure at first, but full of everything they'd left unsaid for years. It was the kind of kiss that quieted the world, that anchored them to a moment they'd carry for the rest of their lives.

Afterward, James rested his forehead against hers. "I should've done that years ago."

Clara smiled through the tears she didn't let fall. "I'm glad you waited."

The following week, James drove to Nashville with his father to officially enlist.

He told Clara the night before he left, sitting with her in the old swing on her porch, their hands clasped tightly like children afraid to be separated in a crowd.

"I'll be in basic training by early June," he said. "Then deployment. Could be North Africa. Maybe Italy. No way to know."

Clara nodded, swallowing hard. "Do you want me to write you?"

"I want you to write me every day," he said. "Even if you think it's nothing. Tell me what the river looks like. What you're reading. What you dreamed about. I want to feel like I'm home when I hear your voice in ink."

She leaned her head on his shoulder. "Then I will."

Graduation came on a day soaked in sunshine.

The gymnasium was filled to the rafters with proud families, church hats, and the sound of camera shutters. Banners hung from the rafters, and the scent of carnations lingered in the air as the senior class filed in, all blue robes and nervous energy. Clara's hands trembled as she clutched her program, scanning the list of names until she found them—Evans, Clara Marie and Whitaker, James Lewis.

When they called her name, Clara walked the stage with grace, her chin high, her heart pounding in her chest. The applause swelled behind her, but all she could hear was the memory of James's voice and the unspoken countdown ticking beneath her skin.

He was just a few names behind her. When he stepped across the stage, her breath caught. There was something about seeing him like that—tall, composed, the tassel brushing his shoulder—that made her heart ache with pride and sorrow all at once.

After the ceremony, the town gathered in the square. It was tradition—lemonade served in mason jars, peach pies lined on long tables, a local trio playing swing music on a makeshift stage. It could have been any other year, but everyone knew it wasn't. Too many boys were wearing dress shirts and new boots. Too many mothers clutched their sons' arms a little too tightly. The war wasn't knocking anymore. It had stepped through the front door.

James found Clara near the edge of the crowd, beneath the tall elm tree where they used to read as children. He was holding something behind his back.

"Close your eyes," he said.

Clara smiled, doing as he asked.

When she opened them, he was holding a delicate necklace—a simple chain with a tiny silver ring threaded through the center. It was his class ring.

"For when I'm gone," he said.

Her fingers trembled as he fastened it around her neck. "James…"

"I want you to wear it," he said gently. "It's yours now."

She looked up at him, her eyes swimming. "This isn't goodbye yet."

"No," he said. "Not yet."

The train was set to leave at dawn.

The Columbia depot was quieter than usual that morning. A few other boys were boarding the same train, some with parents at their sides, others standing alone with stiff backs and trembling lips. Clara stood with James on the platform, her coat pulled tight around her. The air was cool and still, the sky pale and waiting for sun.

James wore his new uniform—khaki pressed, cap tucked neatly under his arm. He looked like a soldier now. Not a boy from next door. Not the boy who built tree forts and kissed her by the river. But somehow, he was both.

Neither of them spoke for a while.

"Do you remember the first time we met?" Clara finally asked, her voice barely audible over the train's soft hiss.

"You mean when you told me I was rude for throwing rocks at frogs?"

She laughed through the tears she had tried to hold back all morning. "You were rude."

"And you were bossy."

"I still am."

James grinned. "Thank God for that."

The conductor called for final boarding. James turned to her then, taking both her hands in his.

"I don't know what's going to happen," he said. "I don't know where I'm going or how long I'll be gone. But I do know one thing."

Clara nodded, blinking fast.

"I love you, Clara Evans. I've loved you since before I knew what love meant."

She reached up, resting her hand on his cheek. "And I'll be loving you long after you come home."

They kissed, slow and full of everything they couldn't say out loud.

When they pulled apart, James pressed a small folded envelope into her palm.

"Don't open it until I'm gone," he whispered. Then he turned, stepping onto the train.

Clara stood rooted to the platform as the whistle blew and the train began to pull away. She watched until it disappeared down the track, a ribbon of smoke trailing into the rising sun.

Only then did she open the letter.

Inside, in James's familiar handwriting, were three simple words:

"Until I return."

Chapter Two: Summer of Us

The summer after James left felt slower than any Clara had ever known.

The days stretched long and heavy, as if time itself refused to move forward without him. Columbia bloomed in its usual way—sunlight warming the sidewalks, flowers bursting along the fences, screen doors creaking open and shut—but for Clara, the world had dimmed. It was as though someone had turned down the color, made the air a little heavier, the sky a little less blue.

She kept busy, or tried to. She worked part-time at the town library, shelving books and dusting reading tables. The older women, kind in their pity, offered her gentle smiles and warm peach cobbler, but Clara didn't want kindness. She wanted James. She wanted his laugh in her kitchen again, his muddy boots by the back door. She wanted to turn toward the sound of the swing creaking on the porch and see him sitting there, carving a stick or reading the sports section with his elbows on his knees.

Instead, there was quiet.

And the letters.

She began writing the same day he left.

June 5, 1942

Dearest James,

I stood on the platform until I couldn't see the train anymore. I told myself I'd walk away once it disappeared, but my feet didn't believe me. The conductor had to ask if I was alright. I told him yes, but it wasn't true. Mama made biscuits this morning. She saved the last one for you out of habit. Then she looked down at her hands like they didn't belong to her. I wore your ring today. I'll wear it every day.

Write when you can. I miss you already.

Always,

Clara

She mailed a letter nearly every day, whether she heard back or not. The mailbox became sacred, a vessel of possibility. Every creak of its door made her heart jump.

By late June, she finally received his first reply.

June 19, 1942

My Clara,

I've read your letter five times already. They gave us only fifteen minutes tonight, but I spent them all on you.
Boot camp is… something. I'll tell you more when I can, but know that I think of you every morning before drills and every night when my feet stop aching.

Tell your mama I miss her biscuits. And you—I miss you like breath.

Always,

James

Reading his words was like touching something real again. She pressed the letter to her chest and cried alone on her bed, then read it three more times beneath the covers, her flashlight casting soft circles on the page.

The rest of the summer passed in chapters—measured not by days or holidays, but by the rhythm of envelopes arriving from faraway posts.

On the surface, life continued. Clara helped her mother tend the garden. She sewed a dress from scratch for the first time.

She joined the Women's Volunteer Committee, though she rarely spoke during meetings, unsure how to explain that her silence came not from weakness, but from the ache of missing someone who was now living in the margins of a map.

Some evenings, she'd take her bike out to Marrowbone Lake alone. She'd sit on the dock where she and James once dangled their legs into the water, sketchbook resting in her lap, pages filled with drawings of uniforms, rifles, and faces she imagined he saw. Sometimes, she'd draw James himself—his jaw clenched in concentration, his hands clasped behind his back, the tilt of his cap just so.

She never showed them to anyone.

Clara often found herself moving through the town as if sleepwalking.

She would drift through the aisles of the general store, reaching for items she didn't need. At church, she sang hymns without hearing her own voice. She listened politely when people asked about James, nodded when they told her how proud she must be. Sometimes she smiled. Most times, she didn't.

Every evening, she lit the porch lantern and sat on the swing. It had been part of her routine since childhood, but now it was different—sacred. That porch had seen her grow, seen her cry, seen her fall in love. Now it bore the weight of waiting.

She would sit there long after her parents went to bed, letters clutched in her lap, the night breeze tugging softly at her hair. The crickets sang their songs, the moon arced overhead, and Clara counted the days in silence.

It wasn't that she doubted James's return.

She simply didn't know how to live in a world where he was gone.

One night in early July, the air thick with heat, Clara curled up in bed and allowed herself to drift back to a memory she hadn't touched in weeks—one of their last summer days together before he enlisted.

It had been a Sunday.

After church, instead of going home, James had grabbed her hand and led her down the back road toward Marrowbone Lake. He didn't say where they were going, but Clara didn't need to ask. She knew the way by heart—the path carved through tall grass and blackberry brambles, the scent of cedar, the hum of dragonflies.

When they reached the edge of the lake, James spread out a blanket and pulled a small paper sack from his satchel.

"I stole these from the church kitchen," he whispered.

Clara gasped. "You didn't."

He grinned. "Mrs. Hollis was distracted. Something about her lemon meringue collapsing."

He handed her a wrapped biscuit and a tiny jar of preserves. They sat side by side, eating in silence, the kind of silence that doesn't need to be filled.

After a while, Clara kicked off her shoes and waded into the water. It was cold and clear, the kind of water that made you feel more awake just by standing in it.

"Come on," she called over her shoulder.

James shook his head. "Not dressed for it."

"You're never dressed for anything. That's never stopped you before."

He rolled his eyes, stripped down to his undershirt, and followed her in, splashing so hard she shrieked and splashed him right back. They played like children, like they had a thousand times before—but something about it felt heavier, more urgent. The laughter was the same, but underneath it was the knowledge that they were nearing the edge of something irreversible.

Later, soaked and shivering on the blanket, James looked over at her and said, "Promise me something."

Clara turned to face him. "Anything."

"Don't wait for me if it hurts too much."

She stared at him, stunned.

"I mean it," he said. "I don't want to be the reason you stop living your life."

Clara reached for his hand, threading her fingers through his. "You don't get to decide that for me."

He nodded slowly, his thumb brushing over her knuckles. "Just… don't forget who you are without me."

She didn't answer then. She only rested her head against his shoulder and memorized the smell of lake water and sun-warmed cotton.

Back in her bed, Clara blinked away the tears that had gathered at the corners of her eyes.

She hadn't forgotten who she was.

But she missed who she was when he was near.

By mid-July, Clara could no longer bear the stillness.

Her grief had settled into something quieter but no less consuming—a dull ache beneath her ribs, a constant sense of absence. She woke each day with the same thought: *Where is he today? Is he safe? Is he thinking of me the way I'm thinking of him?*

So she did what James would've done. She put her hands to work.

She joined the Women's Volunteer Committee full-time, helping with care packages, writing paper drives, and mending old uniforms to be recycled. She learned how to fold gauze for wound dressings and packed tins of coffee and socks into cardboard boxes bound for soldiers overseas. It wasn't glamorous, but it felt like movement—like breathing after weeks of holding her breath.

The other women were kind, though most were older—mothers of boys already deployed. Clara often kept to herself, quiet but dependable, her fingers quick and steady. They never asked much about James. Maybe they didn't need to. The necklace with his ring always hung around her neck, just visible above her blouse.

During breaks, she would sometimes sit at the edge of the room, sipping lemonade, listening to the stories of sons in Italy, brothers in France, husbands somewhere in the Pacific. Every now and then, a letter would be read aloud, and the women would laugh or cry in unison, bound by invisible threads of longing and pride.

Clara never read James's letters aloud. They were hers alone, sacred pieces of a world she didn't want to share.

July 14, 1942

Clara,

Boot camp is like being dropped into the middle of a very loud, very muddy orchestra—where no one's quite sure who's conducting. But we're learning. I'm learning. There's a guy in my unit named Reynolds from Chicago. Loud, fast-talking, always chewing gum. You'd hate him for about three days and then fall in love with his stories. He reminds me that the world is bigger than Tennessee. The food's terrible. The nights are worse. But mornings are kind of beautiful—just before reveille, when the sky turns violet and everything's still. I think of you most then. I miss your voice. I can hear it sometimes when I read your letters.

Please don't stop writing.

Always,

James

She read that letter four times before putting it away.

Afterward, she walked down to the post office, mailed her reply, and stopped by the drugstore for a bottle of ink and a new journal. She was starting to run out of space. Her handwriting had changed slightly since he left—softer, rounder, as though trying to cushion the weight of her emotions.

Her days found rhythm again, measured in chores and letters, tasks and glances toward the sky. She'd write after dinner each night, usually by lamplight in her room, with the hum of the fan in the window and the chirp of crickets outside.

It became more than a routine. It became survival.

July 22, 1942

Dearest James,

Mama says I'm becoming a little too serious these days. She doesn't understand that missing someone you love isn't sadness—it's just a new kind of love, stretched across miles.

Today I helped pack over two dozen care boxes. We filled them with hard candy and soap and playing cards.

I added a note to one—something short and sweet. I like to think it'll make someone smile.

I sat by the river again this afternoon. Drew the clouds. Thought of you.

Come home safe.

Always,

Clara

It was the first week of August when the letter didn't come.

By then, Clara had grown used to the rhythm—two letters a week, sometimes three if James managed to sneak one into the outgoing mail pile between drills. She knew the handwriting by heart. The way he always wrote *Clara* on the front with a slight tilt. The way he signed *Always* like it meant something more than just goodbye.

So when Tuesday came and went without a letter, she told herself it was the weather. When Friday passed with no sign of one either, her heart began to twist.

By the following Tuesday, she was unraveling.

She sat on the porch with the swing still and the ring around her neck clutched tight between her fingers. The mailbox stood quiet at the end of the walkway, a cruel little sentinel that offered nothing but silence.

She tried to distract herself—helped her mother peel peaches, read the newspaper cover to cover, even dusted every corner of the sitting room. But nothing kept her hands from trembling when she thought of what-ifs. Of telegrams. Of mothers crying on their front lawns.

The fear gripped her in the quiet hours, the ones when the town slept and the wind moved like breath through the trees.

Had something happened?

Was he hurt?

Was he—

No. She wouldn't allow the word to form.

That night, she pulled out every letter he'd written and laid them on her bed. Dozens now. Inked in blue and black, some smudged, others torn slightly at the edge. She read each one again, whispering the words as if by speaking them she might conjure his voice.

By the time the sun rose, she was asleep among them.

The letter arrived two days later.

Her hands trembled as she opened it—ripping it slightly in her haste.

August 6, 1942

Clara,

I'm sorry. I didn't mean to make you wait. They moved us without much warning. Everything's changed. I can't say much, but I'm no longer in Georgia. We're preparing for something. They've warned us letters may be delayed from now on.

I hated every day I couldn't write you. Felt like walking without shoes.

There's a chapel here. Small, quiet. I go there sometimes, even though I've never been good at prayers. I sat there the other night and thought of you. Not just the way you look, but how you laugh when you're embarrassed, how you talk to flowers like they can hear you.

You are the best part of me.

Please don't stop writing.

Always,

James

She pressed the letter to her lips and wept.

They weren't tears of grief this time. They were the kind that came after a storm—when the sky cleared, and breath returned, and the world felt possible again.

That night, she walked barefoot down to the river, dress brushing her knees, hair pulled back in a ribbon James had once said reminded him of wildflowers. She sat on the old dock and watched the moon rise over the water.

The fear hadn't disappeared. The war was still very real. But so was her love. So was his voice. And as long as she had those, she still had something to hold onto.

When she returned home, she sat by her window and wrote.

August 7, 1942

My love,

*You didn't break my heart. You made it stronger.
Keep going. Keep holding on. And I will too.*

Always,

Clara

Chapter Three: A Soldier's Oath

The first thing James learned about the Army was that it didn't wait for you to adjust.

Fort Benning greeted him with heat so thick it felt like another layer of skin. The Georgia sun was merciless, and so were the sergeants. By the end of the first day, James's body ached in places he hadn't known could hurt. His uniform clung to him like a wet towel, his boots pinched, and his bunk creaked with every breath he took.

But worse than the physical strain was the noise. Shouting, marching, drills, whistles—everything moved at a volume and pace meant to disorient. The world of Columbia, with its porch swings and slow-spoken charm, felt like a dream he had woken from too quickly.

Still, he didn't complain. He never had.

The second thing he learned was how quickly strangers could become brothers.

There were twenty men in his training unit—boys from Brooklyn and Baton Rouge, from cornfields in Iowa and the copper mines of Arizona. Most of them had never held a rifle before. A few had lied about their age to join. Others, like James, had come because something inside them said they had to.

James bunked beside Reynolds, the fast-talking Chicagoan he'd mentioned in his letter to Clara. Reynolds was sharp, always chewing gum, and cursed with an ease that made the other men laugh. He told wild stories about city girls and subway fights and had a tattoo of an anchor on his left bicep, even though he had never been near the ocean.

At first, James didn't say much. He listened. He observed. But Reynolds took to him anyway.

"You've got that quiet type of grit," he said one night while cleaning his boots. "Like you'd take a bullet just to prove you could."

James chuckled. "Hope I don't have to prove it."

"Don't we all."

Training days were long and grueling.

They ran drills before the sun rose, fired rifles until their shoulders bruised, crawled through mud pits and climbed ropes until their palms tore open. The instructors yelled constantly—correcting, criticizing, demanding more.

James kept his head down and did the work. He wasn't the fastest or the strongest, but he was steady. Focused. And when the others started to lose heart, they often found James already pressing forward, jaw clenched, gaze fixed.

But it wasn't pride that pushed him.

It was Clara.

When the burn in his muscles threatened to break him, he pictured her sitting on the porch swing with her sketchbook in her lap. When the Georgia nights turned cold and the barracks echoed with snores and sobs muffled by blankets, he replayed her voice reading poems by the river. And when they handed him his rifle for the first time—weighty, cold, unfamiliar—he held it like he was holding onto her future.

He hadn't told anyone the full truth. That when he'd said goodbye at the station, it had felt like slicing a piece of himself off. That the part of him that stayed behind in Tennessee was the best part.

He didn't have to tell them.

They knew. Every man there had left something behind. A girl, a mother, a brother, a field. The pain was universal—worn into their hands, scrawled across their letters, soaked into the sweat that stained their uniforms.

On Sundays, they were given an hour of free time.

Most of the men wrote letters, played cards, or slept. James would find a quiet corner of the grounds and sit beneath the trees, pulling out the newest letter from Clara. He read each one slowly, treating them like scripture.

One afternoon, he read a letter that included a small pressed flower—lavender, from the edge of her mother's garden. It was wrapped in wax paper, flattened but still fragrant. He kept it in the same pouch as his identification tags, close to his chest.

He never told the others.

Some things were too sacred to share.

It was called the "Endurance March," though the men had other names for it—less polite, more honest.

Twenty miles. Full packs. Rifles slung across shoulders. No breaks. No exceptions.

They began at dawn, their boots crunching on gravel as the horizon turned from violet to gray. The sergeant walked alongside them for the first half mile, barking orders like a metronome of pain. "Pick it up! Tighten your line! You think the Germans are going to wait for you to catch your breath?"

James kept pace near the center of the group. Reynolds walked beside him, humming a tune under his breath—some jazz rhythm Clara might've liked. It was the only thing keeping James from noticing how much his thighs already burned.

The terrain was unkind. Sunlight baked the dirt roads. Their canteens grew lighter with each mile. The weight of their packs dug into collarbones. The men gritted their teeth and marched on, fueled by nothing more than willpower and fear of being called weak.

By mile twelve, one of the boys from Alabama collapsed. No one stopped. They'd been told what would happen. "You stop, you're out. And you do not want to be *out*."

James bit down hard on the inside of his cheek and kept moving. He thought of Clara, her voice in the letters, her eyes on the platform that day he left. He pictured her sketching the river. He pictured her waiting.

But when they hit mile sixteen, everything in him screamed.

His knees buckled. Blisters bloomed inside his boots. His rifle felt like a block of stone strapped to his back. His breath came in short, ragged gasps, and for the first time since arriving, James felt the edge of failure creeping in.

"I can't—" he muttered.

Reynolds grabbed his sleeve, didn't break stride. "Yes, you can. Just look at my back and keep walking."

James did. He stared at the spot between Reynolds's shoulders and put one foot in front of the other. He didn't think about the pain. He didn't think about the miles ahead. Just that spot. Just Clara.

They crossed the finish line just before sunset.

James collapsed onto the grass, unable to move, lungs raw, vision swimming. The sergeant passed by, gave him a curt nod.

"Good," he grunted. "That's what surviving feels like."

James didn't respond. He couldn't.

But later, after he'd cooled off, after the blisters were cleaned and his feet were bandaged, he sat on his bunk with a letter from Clara in his hands. The envelope smelled faintly of rosemary.

July 31, 1942

My dearest,

I saw a bluebird today. It landed on the porch rail, right in the same spot where we carved our initials when we were kids.

The sky was so bright I had to squint, and for just a moment, I let myself believe you were home again, leaning on the rail beside me.

I keep thinking about what you said. That you're afraid you'll forget how to be the man you were before.

You won't.

That boy who raced me to the mailbox and gave me wildflowers from the field behind your house? He's still there. Even in a uniform. Even in a war.

Come back to me with scars. Come back to me changed.

But just… come back.

Always,
Clara

He read that letter three times that night, then folded it neatly and tucked it under his pillow.

His body still ached.

But his soul—at least for a while—did not.

Graduation from boot camp came with little fanfare—just a handshake from the lieutenant, a set of stripes sewn on the sleeve, and a few claps on the back from his fellow soldiers. But to James, it meant everything.

He had made it.

His blisters had healed, his uniform fit better, and the rifle that once felt foreign now rested easily in his hands. What surprised him most, though, was how the Army had changed his posture—not just physically, but in his sense of self. He stood straighter, moved with more purpose. And yet, when he looked in the mirror, he still saw the same Tennessee boy with dirt in his soul and Clara in his heart.

"You're not the same man who got off that bus in June," Reynolds told him during chow one afternoon.

"I know," James said. "Feels like a lifetime."

"You ready for the next one?"

James paused, his fork halfway to his mouth. "What next one?"

Reynolds leaned in. "Rumor is, we're shipping out in two weeks. Real deployment. Not more training. Real war."

James's stomach tightened.

He'd known it was coming. The whole point of the last few months had been to prepare for this. But hearing it put into words—*real war*—sounded different. Final. Irrevocable.

That night, the sergeant confirmed it. Their unit was being reassigned. They would deploy to North Africa by September.

"Gear up, gentlemen," the sergeant said, pacing in front of the bunkhouse. "You're soldiers now. And soldiers go where they're needed. Your mama's front porch ain't gonna win this war."

Some of the men cheered. Others stood quiet. James felt his chest pull tight—not with fear, but with longing.

He missed the front porch. He missed Clara.

He wrote to her that night.

August 10, 1942

Clara,

I got my stripes today. Squad leader. First thing I did was look for you to tell you. Funny how I still turn my head like you'll be there, even when I know you're miles away.
We're shipping out soon. I can't tell you where yet. But it's real this time.

There's a knot in my stomach that won't go away, and I think it's because I don't know what's waiting for me. All I know is that I want to make it back to you.

When we get our next break, I'll try to call. Hearing your voice, even for a minute, would be enough to carry me across an ocean.

Tell me everything. Tell me something small.

Tell me about the river.

Always,
James

He didn't sleep much that night.

Instead, he lay awake and imagined what the world looked like from Clara's window. The moonlight over Maple Street. The rustle of trees outside her room. The porch swing that groaned just a little louder when it was humid.

Those memories weren't just comfort. They were fuel.

The last two weeks at Fort Benning passed in a blur of orders and equipment checks, paperwork and vaccinations, final rifle drills and long lectures on desert warfare. The men received new uniforms, canvas packs, emergency rations, and maps labeled only with coded coordinates.

At night, James sat by the barracks writing letters faster than the mail could move. He filled entire pages with the small things—his favorite part of the day, a new song someone was whistling in the mess hall, how the stars here didn't feel like Tennessee stars, but he tried to trace constellations anyway.

He told Clara everything he could.

Because soon, there would be so much he wouldn't be allowed to say.

The ship was enormous.

It sat in the harbor like a sleeping giant, gray and silent except for the hiss of steam and the distant creak of its metal belly. Soldiers filed up the gangplank in single file, packs slung over shoulders, rifles cradled like sleeping children. James gripped the railing tightly, the salt wind pulling at his collar, the taste of iron and ocean sharp in his throat.

This was it.

There had been no goodbyes at the dock. No waving handkerchiefs. No last-minute letters. Just orders, duffel bags, and a final salute to American soil. His boots echoed off the steel deck as he made his way to his assigned quarters below. The air smelled of oil and salt and something else—something that reminded him of the old train yard back in Columbia, like movement and waiting and rust.

The ship groaned to life, and James stood at the edge of the deck, eyes fixed on the thinning shoreline behind them. The coast faded slowly, swallowed by haze, until there was only water in every direction.

He'd never seen this much ocean before.

It was beautiful. It was terrifying.

Reynolds leaned on the rail beside him, chewing a stick of gum. "You ever think we'll come back this way?"

James didn't look at him. "I have to."

"Because of her?"

James nodded. "Because of Clara."

Reynolds went quiet for a moment, then said, "That's a good reason."

They stood in silence for a while, the sea rising and falling like breath all around them. Somewhere deep below, the engines thrummed like a heartbeat. James pressed his hand to the front of his jacket, feeling the small bump where Clara's lavender flower still sat, wrapped in wax paper, close to his dog tags.

He thought about the porch swing. About the way she looked the night before graduation. The curve of her smile when she teased him about not wearing socks. The letter that arrived after he nearly collapsed on the endurance march.

She had kept him grounded. Kept him whole.

Now she was the reason he would face whatever came next.

That night, James wrote by flashlight in the narrow bunk he shared with two other soldiers. The ship rocked gently, and he could hear the low murmur of waves outside the porthole.

August 19, 1942

My Clara,

I'm writing this on the ocean. We left yesterday. I can't tell you where we're going or how long it will take, but I can tell you this—it feels like the world has shifted under my feet.
I stood on the deck today and thought of you. Thought of Tennessee. Of home. I promised you I'd come back. I'm keeping that promise.

No matter where they send me, no matter what happens—I will carry you with me.

I will carry you through everything.

Always,
James

The ship moved onward through the night, cutting through the dark Atlantic like a steel arrow loosed from a bow.

James lay awake long after the other men had begun to snore, staring at the ceiling above him and imagining Clara staring at the same moon on the other side of the world.

He reached for the edge of the bunk, found the corner of her last letter folded beneath his pillow, and held it there like prayer.

The world was at war.

But love, he told himself, was still the most powerful thing he knew.

Chapter Four: Ink-Stained Promises

The letter arrived on a Wednesday.

It came folded in its usual way—creased cleanly down the center, her name written in his familiar hand across the envelope's front. But this one was different. The paper was damp from sea air, the ink slightly smudged, and the envelope bore a military stamp she hadn't seen before.

Clara knew, before she opened it, that James was no longer in the country.

Her hands trembled as she slid her finger beneath the flap, carefully preserving the seal. Her heart beat like a war drum in her chest, the breath caught in her throat.

Then she read it.

Each word unfurled like a ribbon of memory, full of longing and bravery, of salt air and love sent across an ocean. He was on the water now—heading somewhere unknown. She could almost see him leaning over the railing of a great ship, his uniform rippling in the wind, her name tucked against his heart like a compass pointing home.

She read the letter once. Then again. Then pressed it to her lips, her tears landing softly on the page.

He had kept his promise. He was still writing.

Life in Columbia was shifting.

The war wasn't just a headline anymore—it was a presence. It crept into everything: ration books, factory shifts, whispered conversations in church pews. Families hung stars in their windows—blue for service, gold for sacrifice. More windows had stars now. More stores were short on sugar, and more evenings ended in prayer.

Clara's mother had taken a second job at the post office. Her father spent evenings listening to the radio, twisting his wedding ring as updates poured in from overseas.

Clara felt the change most in her chest. A low, constant ache.

James's letters continued, but more of them were blacked out now. Whole lines missing—censored by military eyes to protect locations, names, operations. Sometimes she'd receive one that looked like a ghost of what it once was, blank spaces haunting the paragraphs.

Still, she read between the lines.

She learned to hear what wasn't said.

And she wrote him, too—every night without fail. Her letters became the most consistent part of her day. Ink to paper. Heart to page. Her love stitched into every loop of cursive.

August 24, 1942

My James,

I walked to the lake today and sat on the dock in the same place we watched the fireworks that Fourth of July before senior year. The air was warm and still, and for a moment, I could almost believe you were there beside me, your hand in mine, your laughter chasing fireflies into the night. But you're not here. You're out there, somewhere I can't follow, and that truth clings to me like mist.

But I write you because it makes me feel like I'm doing something. Like I'm fighting in my own way.

Come back to me.

Always,
Clara

In town, she volunteered more. Sewing bandages, sorting clothes, folding paper cranes with the schoolchildren to send in care packages. She spoke little, worked quickly, and thought of James constantly.

She started a scrapbook, too.

It wasn't much—a simple leather-bound journal with a broken clasp—but she filled it with clippings, sketches, pressed flowers, pieces of ribbon, and words that reminded her of him. Quotes from novels. Lyrics from the radio. Doodles of things they'd seen together. One page read simply:

"The porch still creaks. I still sit there. And I still love you."

September came with a coolness in the air that Clara usually loved.

But this year, it felt more like a warning.

The letter didn't arrive on Tuesday. Or Wednesday. Or the entire week after.

She waited by the mailbox each afternoon, fingers twisting the chain around her neck, scanning every car that passed the corner, hoping the postman might slow, might smile, might lift a hand with that precious envelope.

But nothing came.

She told herself it was delays. Transport schedules. Storms at sea. Anything but the thing she truly feared. She still smiled at the neighbors. Still helped her mother fold laundry and sweep the front steps. But at night, when the house went quiet, she sat on the floor by her bed and cried into her hands like the girl she hadn't let herself be since James left.

The silence became a weight. A punishment. She thought of every goodbye they had shared—every letter she had ever sent—and wondered if it had been enough.

Had he read her last one?

Had he made it?

Her thoughts grew darker with each day that passed. She imagined telegrams. Military officers on doorsteps. Her name etched on a list somewhere, beside a number she didn't want to understand.

It wasn't until the following Thursday that someone knocked on the door.

It wasn't a soldier.

It was Mrs. Jennings, the librarian, holding a small bundle of mail wrapped in twine. "Clara, dear," she said gently, "the post office accidentally filed some of these in the wrong box. I think this one's for you."

Clara took the bundle with shaking hands, eyes scanning for his handwriting. And then—there it was.

Whitaker, James L.
Still in his neat, deliberate script.

She didn't even wait to thank Mrs. Jennings properly. She just nodded, stepped back into the house, and dropped onto the nearest chair as she tore it open.

September 3, 1942

My Clara,

I'm okay. I know this letter is late and I know you're probably tearing your hair out worrying, but please believe me—I'm still here.

We moved again. New place, hotter than the last. The days blur together—training, marching, building trenches. The real kind now.

I saw a boy get his first letter from home today. His hands shook like mine did the first time your name showed up in my mail. He cried. I didn't tease him.

You'd be proud of me. I'm leading five men now. I give orders. I check maps. Sometimes I miss being the quiet one who followed.

But every time I doubt myself, I think of you.

Please don't stop writing. Your letters are the one thing that still feels like home.

Always,
James

Clara laughed through her tears.

She pressed the letter to her lips and let the joy of it wash over her. Not because he was poetic or wrote anything particularly grand. But because he was still alive. Still writing. Still *hers*.

That Sunday, she wore her navy blue dress to church—the one James had said brought out the color of her eyes. She walked to her pew with quiet confidence, and for the first time in weeks, she sang every hymn. Not just with her lips—but from the center of her chest, where hope had been slowly blooming back to life.

After the service, Mrs. Jennings found her again and handed her a small envelope.

"This one arrived this morning," she said. "From the military. Official, but not bad."

Clara opened it on the church steps.

Inside was a certificate. James Whitaker, Squad Leader – Commendation of Conduct. A note was tucked in with it, explaining that families of soldiers who had received field promotions or leadership recognition would be notified accordingly.

Clara stared at the paper, then smiled to herself.

She wasn't surprised.

He had always been a leader.

He just didn't know it yet.

The photograph came folded inside a letter, thin and black-and-white, tucked between two pages of ink.

Clara hadn't expected it. The envelope looked like the others—creased, smudged by travel, James's handwriting neat and tight along the front. But this time, it held something more than just words.

She unfolded the paper slowly, careful not to tear.

There he was.

James stood in front of a canvas army tent, hands on his hips, squinting slightly into the sun. He looked older, sharper somehow—his jaw more defined, his shoulders broader. There was dirt on his uniform, a shadow of fatigue beneath his eyes, but his smile was the same.

Steady. Quietly proud. Entirely *him.*

Behind him, a few other men lounged on crates and makeshift benches, one holding a cigarette, another mid-laugh. James stood a little apart—close, but apart—as if he carried something heavier, something unspoken. Clara wondered if the others knew how often he thought of home, if they understood that part of his heart lived in the letters he tucked into his rucksack every night.

She stared at the photo for nearly an hour.

Traced the lines of his boots. The curve of his arm. The tiny smudge on the corner that might've been a fingerprint from the man who developed it.

Then she placed it in her scrapbook, just above a sketch she had drawn of the two of them fishing at the lake, years ago.

Beneath it, she wrote in careful cursive:

"Still mine. Still him."

That week, the town clinic put out a call for volunteers.

Columbia, like everywhere else, was running thin—on supplies, on staff, on time. Several nurses had joined the war effort, and the clinic needed help with basic care: washing linens, sorting medications, escorting patients between rooms.

Clara hesitated at first.

She wasn't a nurse. She wasn't studying medicine. But something pulled at her—a quiet tug just beneath her ribs that said *go.* Maybe it was the way her hands had steadied when folding bandages. Or the way she had memorized James's symptoms from his letters—blisters, fever, aching shoulders—and imagined how she might help if she were near.

So she signed up.

The first day was simple. She folded gowns, filled water pitchers, took notes for Mrs. Keene, the head nurse. The second day, she helped a young boy wrap a burn he got trying to cook breakfast for his siblings.

By the end of the week, Clara found herself staying late, asking questions, wanting to know more.

There was something calming about it—doing work that mattered. Easing pain. Reassuring frightened children. Carrying trays down hushed hallways. She felt useful in a way she hadn't since James left.

One afternoon, Mrs. Keene pulled her aside in the hallway.

"You've got good instincts," she said, wiping her hands on her apron. "You ever thought about nursing?"

Clara blinked. "No… not really."

"Maybe you should. You've got a steady heart. That's rare."

Clara smiled softly, uncertain. "I'm not sure what I have. Except a boy who's very far away."

"Then do it for him," Mrs. Keene said. "Or for you."

Clara didn't answer right away.

But that night, she sat by the window with the photograph of James on her lap and let herself imagine—just for a moment—what it might feel like to see him again, not as a girl who had waited, but as a woman who had grown strong in his absence.

The decision didn't come in a flash.

It came slowly, like the sun creeping up behind the Tennessee hills. One moment of certainty followed by another. Then another. Until it was undeniable.

Clara Evans was going to be a nurse.

It started with how her hands moved over patients' bandages—gentle but firm. The way she instinctively calmed the nervous children who came into the clinic clutching their mother's hands. The way she remembered every detail of James's letters—how long he marched, how cold the nights got, how tired his feet were. She began studying field medic manuals borrowed from the library, copying diagrams and first aid instructions into a spare journal. She wanted to know what he was going through.

She wanted to be prepared if he ever came home wounded.

One evening, she stayed after hours helping Mrs. Keene organize supplies. The clinic was quiet except for the soft ticking of a wall clock and the hum of the floor fan. Outside, crickets chirped and fireflies blinked in the dusk.

"You're serious about this," Mrs. Keene said, gently folding a bloodied towel.

Clara nodded. "I think I've been serious for a while. I just didn't have the words."

The older woman offered a soft smile. "Then get your paperwork in order. If you want to start training here officially, I'll vouch for you."

Clara's throat tightened. "Thank you."

"Don't thank me. Just don't stop."

That night, Clara sat by the open window in her bedroom, the moonlight spilling across her desk. She lit a lamp, pulled out a fresh sheet of stationery, and began to write the most important letter of her life so far.

September 12, 1942

My James,

I think I found my place.

I've started helping at the clinic here in Columbia. At first it was just small things—bandages, bedsheets, taking notes—but now I'm training. Mrs. Keene thinks I have potential. I think I just want to understand the kind of strength you show every day.

This war has taken so much. But it's also given me something. A path. A reason.

I want to be someone who stands beside others when they're hurting. I want to help people come home. I want to help you come home.

I'm not the same girl who kissed you on the riverbank that spring. I hope when you return, you'll still recognize me—changed, but still yours.

I miss you every second.

I love you more with each breath.

Always,
Clara

She sealed the envelope and held it to her chest before placing it in the outbox on her windowsill. The wind moved gently through the curtains, and somewhere in the night, an owl called out across the fields.

She imagined James in a distant land—perhaps already stepping through sand, or preparing in a canvas tent under foreign stars—and hoped, with every fiber of her being, that her words would reach him.

That he would know he wasn't walking this war alone.

That while he carried a rifle, she would carry a lamp. A basin. A pair of steady hands.

She would be ready for him.

Not just to welcome him home…

But to help him heal.

Chapter Five: Her Call to Serve

Clara stood on the platform of the Nashville train station with a suitcase in one hand and her acceptance letter in the other.

The letter was already worn at the edges from how often she'd unfolded it:

"The Army Nurse Corps accepts your application for initial training and assignment. Report to Camp Forrest, Tullahoma, Tennessee—October 5, 1942."

Even in her new gray coat, even with her hair pinned in careful curls, she felt smaller than she had in years. The world was moving faster now. No longer the steady rhythm of Columbia and porch swings and handwritten letters. This was motion. Purpose. Something bigger.

"Are you nervous?" her mother had asked that morning, brushing invisible lint from Clara's coat as they stood by the doorway.

"Yes," she had admitted, pressing her lips into a tight line.

"Good," her mother had said. "That means it matters."

Now, as the train pulled into the station with a shriek of brakes and a plume of steam, Clara lifted her chin and stepped forward.

Camp Forrest was a sprawling sea of barracks, tents, and mud.

Women from all over the South had gathered for training—some already nurses, others like Clara, eager and untested. She was assigned a bunk in a long, drafty hall with twenty other girls. The air smelled of starch and soap, and the only personal touches were the occasional family photo tacked above a bed or a Bible tucked beneath a pillow.

They wore uniforms now—dove gray dresses with matching caps and dark leather shoes. Clara studied herself in the mirror the first morning, running a hand along the crisp edge of her collar. She barely recognized the woman staring back.

Then she picked up her bag and joined the others outside.

Training began at sunrise and didn't end until the stars blinked back into the sky. They learned how to apply tourniquets in less than twenty seconds, how to sterilize scalpels, how to carry stretchers without losing balance. They drilled in military protocol, took courses in anatomy and field trauma, and spent entire afternoons learning how to triage under pressure.

Clara took notes furiously. Practiced longer than anyone else. Asked questions when no one else would.

On the third day, a sergeant watched her dress a deep laceration on a practice dummy and said, "You've got field hands. That's good. We don't need delicate. We need fast and clean."

It was the closest thing to a compliment she'd received all week.

At night, Clara wrote to James.

Her letters were shorter now, more focused. Less poetry, more truth. She didn't write about the weather or the color of the leaves anymore. She wrote about patients. About bandages. About how she'd learned to find a pulse under pressure. She wanted him to know she was changing, not drifting.

October 8, 1942

James,

They taught us how to stabilize broken ribs today. We practiced with a dummy that didn't look like a person, but I imagined it was someone I cared about.

I imagined it was you.

This isn't easy work, but it feels right. Like I was supposed to be here all along, I just didn't know it.

I miss your words. I miss your laugh. But most of all, I miss your silence. That peaceful, steady quiet you carried around like armor.

I hope you're still holding on to it.

Always,
Clara

The first time Clara heard a man scream in pain, her hands froze.

It was late October, and she had been assigned to the surgical ward at the Camp Forrest field hospital for the final stage of training. Most patients were U.S. soldiers injured during maneuvers—broken arms, shrapnel cuts, heatstroke—but some had just returned from real battle zones. They were the ones who looked through people rather than at them.

Clara had just stepped into the hallway, carrying a tray of gauze and antiseptic, when the sound erupted from the room down the hall. A young man—barely older than James—was being treated for a deep leg wound. He had taken mortar shrapnel to the thigh and was refusing morphine.

"No more," he gasped, teeth clenched. "No more medicine—I need to feel it. I need to stay awake."

The nurse beside him was trying to hold him steady while the doctor worked. Blood pooled on the floor.

Clara stood in the doorway, frozen, the tray trembling in her hands.

"Evans!" someone barked. "Help us with pressure—now!"

Clara moved on instinct. She dropped to her knees beside the soldier, placed both hands on the cloth pressing into the wound, and leaned her weight into it. Blood soaked through her sleeves. The smell of iron filled her nose. The young man gripped her wrist so tightly she thought the bones might snap.

But she didn't let go.

Not until the bleeding slowed. Not until the morphine finally took hold and the boy stopped shaking.

Later, scrubbing her arms in the nurse's washroom, she stared at the bloodstains on her uniform.

It was the first time she truly understood what it meant to serve—not just in title, but in spirit.

That night, she didn't write to James right away.

She sat alone on her bunk, arms sore, her heart heavy in a way she didn't know how to describe. She thought of James in trenches somewhere, of men screaming beside him, of what he must have already seen. What he might have already done.

Her hands had touched blood now.

Not ink. Not pages.

Blood.

She finally wrote, simply:

October 22, 1942

James,

I thought I was ready. I wasn't. But I didn't run.

I'm still here.

And I still love you.

Always,
Clara

His response came a week later—longer than usual. The envelope was bent, the edges frayed. The postmark had been smeared by rain or seawater.

When she opened it, the handwriting startled her.

It was still James's, but shakier. Slanted. The ink uneven.

October 30, 1942

Clara,

We were under fire for the first time. Real fire. Real death.
I don't know how to write about it. I don't know if I should.

One of my men—his name was Lawrence—was hit beside me. I held his hand. I told him he was going to be okay. But he wasn't.

Afterward, I couldn't speak. I just walked until someone pulled me down into the trench and told me to sleep.

But I couldn't.

I dreamed of you instead.

Not in a field. Not in uniform. Just you, laughing by the river, hair in the wind, your hands drawing flowers in a notebook.

I think that memory kept me from breaking.

So I'm writing you now, even though I feel like someone else wrote this.

Please don't stop. Please don't stop writing.

You're the only thing that reminds me I'm still alive.

Always,
James

Clara pressed the letter to her chest and didn't move for a long time.

Tears rolled silently down her cheeks. Not just for him. Not just for Lawrence. But for all of them—for every boy sent into hell with only letters and prayer for armor.

She would write again.

And she would serve harder.

Because James was holding on.

And so would she.

Graduation day came cold and clear.

On November 14, 1942, Clara stood among sixty-eight women dressed in crisp gray uniforms, the red cross stitched over their hearts. Flags flanked the platform. A brass band played softly. And for the first time in weeks, Clara felt the weight of something sacred settling on her shoulders—not grief or fear, but purpose.

They had marched for weeks. Memorized field protocols. Pulled double shifts in the hospital wing. Watched men die. Saved others. And now, they stood straight-backed in formation, waiting to hear what came next.

Colonel Adams, a stern woman with iron-gray hair and an even firmer voice, stepped up to the podium.

"You have completed your training," she said. "You are no longer students. You are now Army nurses. You will go where you are needed. You will see things that cannot be unseen. And you will carry hope into places where it has long been forgotten. That is your charge."

The ceremony was brief. Names were called. Orders were distributed. Papers were handed out with locations that made Clara's stomach twist—Casablanca, London, Tunisia.

When she opened her envelope, her hands shook.

"Assignment: 8th Evacuation Hospital – Italy."

She read it three times.

Italy.

It was the same region James had mentioned months ago. He hadn't been able to say much—only vague references to "southern terrain" and "movement across the peninsula"—but Clara had remembered.

Now, she was going there too.

That night, she sat alone at the edge of her bunk, clutching her orders and the latest letter from James.

November 9, 1942

Clara,

The days are blurring now. I don't know where we are half the time. I only know it's cold and muddy and loud.
We lost another. But we also held the line. And sometimes, that's the best thing we can do—just hold.

I've started writing your name in the margins of my notebook. Over and over. Sometimes I don't even realize I'm doing it. Just… Clara Clara Clara.

There's talk of movement soon. No one knows where. I just pray we're not pushed into something worse.

Tell me you're still out there. Tell me something good.

Always,
James

Clara smiled through her tears.

"Tell me something good."

She took out her pen, heart pounding.

November 14, 1942

James,

Here's something good: I graduated today. I'm officially an Army nurse, and I just received my orders. I'm being sent to Italy.

Italy, James.

I don't know where you are exactly—I know you can't say—but maybe... maybe we'll be closer than we've been in months.

Maybe fate still has a thread holding us together.

I'll be brave. I promise.

But please, if you're still holding on, hold tighter. Because

I'm coming.

Always,
Clara

A week later, Clara stood at the edge of another train platform—this time bound for the East Coast, where she would board a military transport ship with dozens of other nurses.

Her parents stood beside her. Her mother held back tears. Her father shook her hand like she was one of the soldiers he used to serve with.

"You come home, Clara Marie," her father said, gripping her hand tighter. "No matter what, you come home."

Clara looked at them both and nodded. "I will."

She carried one bag, one book, and one photograph of James tucked into her Bible.

The train pulled away slowly, smoke rising behind it like a promise fading into the sky.

The ship groaned as it cut through waves taller than most houses in Columbia.

It wasn't like James had described in his letters. For Clara, the Atlantic crossing was cold, crowded, and wet. Below deck, the air was thick with the smell of diesel fuel and sea salt, mixed with the occasional waft of motion sickness. Nurses bunked in tight quarters, four to a room the size of a garden shed.

She didn't mind.

Every night, she stood on the deck, gripping the rail with gloved hands, eyes fixed on the horizon. Somewhere out there, on another patch of land, James was still breathing. That was enough to keep her steady.

When they reached Gibraltar, the ship stopped briefly before moving into the Mediterranean. The coastlines changed. The air warmed. And then, at last—Italy.

The port was bustling with chaos. Trucks rumbled over broken pavement. Soldiers barked orders in English and Italian. Planes soared overhead, and sand clung to everything. Clara stepped off the transport and into the red clay dust of war.

She was assigned to a field hospital near Bari, a small city on the Adriatic coast. The 8th Evacuation Hospital was built hastily in an olive grove—rows of olive drab tents flapping in the wind, generators buzzing in the background. The tents smelled of antiseptic and sweat. Cots lined the canvas walls. Wounded men arrived by the dozen.

Clara went to work immediately.

There was no time to adjust. Within hours, she was dressing wounds, checking vitals, translating basic instructions for Italian civilians, and comforting soldiers whose faces were too young for the things their eyes had seen.

At night, she washed her hands until the smell of blood faded. Sometimes it didn't.

She never asked where the men came from. Not directly. But sometimes, one of them would mention a nearby battalion number or speak the name of a town James had once written about. Those moments made her breath catch.

He was close. He had to be.

December 2, 1942

James,

I'm in Italy now. The tents are dusty, the food is strange, and the sky looks nothing like Tennessee's.

But I'm working. And I'm helping.

They assigned me to a surgical tent. We receive casualties around the clock. Some from places I know you've been.

One man mentioned a ridge near San Giovanni.

I didn't ask questions. I just listened.

Please write if you can. Just a word. Just my name.
Even if you're only a few hills away, it would mean everything to know you're still here.

Always,
Clara

Three nights later, she was awoken by a soldier shouting outside her tent. A transport had arrived. Twelve new wounded.

Clara pulled on her boots and coat, still half asleep, and ran toward the triage line. The smell of metal hit her first—fresh blood. Then came the sound—groans, shouting, the squeak of stretchers.

She took her place beside Dr. Lively, who handed her gloves without looking up. "Two chest wounds. One leg amputation. Multiple shrapnel injuries. Start IVs and prep for surgery."

Clara moved on instinct now. Pressure here. Clamp there. Whisper words of comfort where she could. One soldier reached for her hand. His was burned raw. She held it anyway.

Hours passed.

The sun began to rise.

And still, she worked.

By morning, she had collapsed into a chair outside the tent. Her hands were raw. Her feet throbbed. Her back screamed. But she didn't cry.

Not because she wasn't scared. Not because she didn't feel it. But because something inside her had shifted—had strengthened.

She was no longer the girl who waited by a mailbox.

She was here.

She was part of this.

And she was ready to keep going.

Because somewhere beyond the trees, beyond the hills and wreckage and gunfire, James Whitaker was still out there.

And she had made a vow:

She would find him.

Chapter Six: Training Grounds

The days began to blend.

Each morning, Clara woke to the buzz of generators, the flapping of canvas, and the scent of wet earth and iodine. Her fingers ached from gripping forceps. Her legs burned from long hours on her feet. But she didn't complain.

This—exhausting, relentless, and raw—was what she had come for.

In the surgical tents, time had its own rhythm. One minute a soldier was brought in with a bullet in his abdomen, screaming for his mother. The next, he was unconscious, rushed to surgery, and Clara was holding a lantern above the operating table, praying the blood didn't stain too deep.

She had learned to work quickly. Wash wounds. Monitor morphine doses. Write casualty tags with a hand that never trembled. But she never stopped listening—especially when the soldiers talked in half-delirious murmurs. That was when the truth came out.

"You from Tennessee?" one man asked her as she cleaned the dried blood from his collarbone.

She paused. "Yes. Columbia."

"My captain's from Tennessee. Whitaker. James, I think. Quiet guy. Good shot."

Clara's breath caught. Her hand froze over the gauze.

"Where did you serve with him?" she asked, trying to sound calm.

The soldier squinted. "Mountains. Couple months ago. He rotated east. Think he got reassigned near the front."

That was all he said before the morphine pulled him under.

It was enough.

He was alive.

Clara spent the rest of the night writing his name over and over in her journal:

James Whitaker – reassigned east.

The nurses in her unit became family.

There was Nora, from Pittsburgh, who had a wicked sense of humor and a locket with her fiancé's photo tucked inside her boot. Evelyn, the oldest of the group, who had served in Spain and never flinched—not even when a man lost his arm in front of her. And Marie, from New Orleans, who spoke three languages and cried when she saw children begging outside the gates.

They shared everything—letters, rations, combs, fears. At night, they wrote by flashlight or shared coffee warmed over portable burners. Sometimes, they just sat in silence, staring up at the Italian sky, wondering what the stars looked like back home.

Clara didn't say much about James. Only that he was a squad leader, and that she was hoping—*no, expecting*—to see him again.

"Men get moved around a lot," Evelyn warned gently. "Don't lose yourself chasing ghosts."

"He's not a ghost," Clara replied, her voice steady. "He's a promise."

On her next day off, Clara visited the quartermaster's tent and asked for a list of nearby infantry units. The sergeant behind the desk raised an eyebrow.

"You looking for someone?" he asked.

Clara nodded. "Yes. James Whitaker. Squad leader. Tennessee infantry."

The man whistled. "Sorry, miss. We don't keep individual troop records here. Closest I can tell you is that elements of the 36th moved northeast three weeks ago. Maybe toward San Pietro."

"San Pietro," she repeated, writing it down.

"Why him?" the sergeant asked, curiosity plain on his face.

Clara slipped her notebook back into her pocket. "Because he's mine."

The request raised eyebrows.

Nurses weren't supposed to ask for reassignments—especially not to posts closer to the front. But Clara didn't care about expectations. She had already faced blood, fear, and death. She was ready for more if it meant getting even a few miles closer to James.

She brought her transfer papers to Major Leland, the logistics officer, and waited while he reviewed them beneath the dim light of a kerosene lamp.

"You want to go *closer* to the fighting?" he asked flatly, looking up from her form.

"Yes, sir."

"Why?"

"I believe I can be more useful there. I've worked triage in active zones. I've assisted in surgeries. And—" she paused, "—I believe someone I know may be stationed nearby."

The major's gaze narrowed. "This someone wouldn't happen to be a particular soldier, would he?"

Clara didn't blink. "Yes, sir. A squad leader. James Whitaker, 36th Infantry. He was rotated east toward San Pietro. That's where I want to go."

He leaned back, tapping his pen on the desk. "You understand this is not about sentiment. It's about placement."

"I understand that completely."

After a long moment, he sighed. "We're short on nurses near San Pietro Ridge. That sector is rough terrain—mountain passes, snipers, artillery every day. If you're looking for comfort, you won't find it there."

"I'm not looking for comfort, Major. I'm looking for service."

Another pause.

Then: "Request approved."

She was transferred three days later.

The journey north took nearly a day—through winding roads, past crumbled villages and burned-out tanks. Clara rode in the back of a transport truck with two medics and a crate of morphine. The air grew colder with each mile, the terrain steeper. Gunfire echoed faintly in the distance, distant thunder in the bones of the mountains.

When they arrived at the forward field unit—a tent hospital hastily erected in a stone monastery—Clara barely had time to breathe before she was put to work.

There were no beds here. Only stretchers. No running water. No electricity beyond a few scattered lanterns and portable generators.

This wasn't medicine.

This was survival.

Her second night there brought a test she wasn't ready for.

Two soldiers were carried in at once.

One was a young enlisted private, unconscious, bleeding from his abdomen. The other, a colonel with a shattered shoulder and a fractured rib.

Only one operating table was available.

Clara and the other nurse—Marie—looked to the surgeon for orders. But the doctor hesitated. "Triage protocol," he said, quietly. "Stabilize the colonel. Prioritize rank."

Clara's blood went cold.

"The private is critical," she argued. "If we wait, he'll bleed out."

"The colonel gives the orders that save a hundred other lives."

Marie stared at the floor.

Clara stared at the boy.

He couldn't have been more than nineteen.

She clenched her jaw, heart racing. "We don't treat uniforms. We treat humans."

The doctor snapped, "We treat *what we're told to treat*."

Clara stepped back, swallowing the protest on her tongue. She wanted to scream. She wanted to shove past them and save the private herself. But her hands didn't move.

Not yet.

Instead, she knelt beside the boy, pressed her hand to his wrist, and whispered into his ear.

"I see you. I'm sorry. I'm so sorry."

His pulse flickered. Then faded.

He died quietly on the floor while the colonel was prepped for surgery.

That night, Clara sat alone beneath a cypress tree at the monastery's edge, her hands still stained, her chest aching with rage.

She didn't write a letter.

She didn't cry.

She just stared into the darkness and promised herself that if she ever found James again, she would not let bureaucracy be the thing that took him from her.

Not while she still had breath in her lungs.

The monastery turned field hospital sat at the foot of the San Pietro ridge—where the air was sharp and the sound of distant shelling never stopped.

Clara kept her focus on the work. But her mind was always listening—always searching.

Every wounded man who passed through her hands became a possible lead.

"Do you know a James Whitaker?" she'd ask gently, after bandaging wounds or easing pain.

Most shook their heads.

Some simply didn't remember anything at all.

But one afternoon, in a moment when Clara had almost stopped asking, a voice croaked from a cot near the rear of the tent.

"Yeah," the man rasped. "I know Whitaker."

Clara froze.

He was gaunt, wrapped in a thermal blanket, an IV dripping into his arm. His right leg was heavily bandaged. His dog tags read: Mitchell, E. A.

Clara approached slowly. "You served with him?"

Mitchell nodded. "Thirty-sixth. Bravo Company. Hill 112. Two weeks ago."

Her breath caught.

"Is he—was he—okay?"

Mitchell gave a weak smile. "He's the reason I'm not in a box right now. Took shrapnel to the leg. I was screaming like a fool, bleeding out. Everyone else kept moving. Orders were to push. But Whitaker? He turned back. Dragged me a hundred yards to safety."

Clara's knees nearly gave out.

"He saved you?"

"Yeah," Mitchell whispered. "Quiet guy. But solid. The kind of man you'd follow into hell."

She swallowed hard, her voice barely audible. "Do you know where he went after?"

Mitchell closed his eyes. "They split the unit. I heard his team moved east. Toward the Liri Valley. That's all I know."

Liri Valley.

Another name. Another thread.

Clara squeezed his hand. "Thank you. For telling me."

"Wait," Mitchell murmured. "Are you his wife?"

She smiled faintly. "Not yet."

Later that night, Clara sat on her cot and traced the route on a map she had marked in her journal. From the monastery to Hill 112. Then east. Toward Liri.

Each name, each ridge and river, brought her closer.

She didn't know when or how she'd find him—but she *would*.

She also finally felt strong enough to write him again.

December 11, 1942

James,

I met someone today. A soldier you carried off a hill. He said you saved him without hesitation. That doesn't surprise me.

You've always been the steady one. The brave one. The one who never lets go.

Now it's my turn.

I'm not far from where you were. I'm working in a monastery near San Pietro. If you're near Liri Valley, we're breathing the same air.

Maybe I'll look up and see you walking toward me any day now.

Until then—I'll be here.

Always,
Clara

Three days later, as the snow began to fall across the hills for the first time that winter, Clara stood outside the tent with her canteen, sipping from it slowly.

In the distance, trucks rumbled toward the hospital. New arrivals.

She braced herself. Another round of bandages, surgeries, pain.

But this time, her heart thudded a little faster.

Because somewhere in those trucks, somewhere on that road—James might be drawing closer.

The order came just after dawn.

The hospital unit was to move east—closer to the fighting near the Gustav Line. German resistance was tightening, and the Allied forces needed medical support near the Liri Valley.

Clara read the relocation notice with numb fingers.

Liri Valley.

It felt like fate was nudging her forward.

They packed in silence. Cots were broken down. Instruments were sterilized and sealed. Stretchers and crates were loaded into trucks. The monastery, which had become a strange kind of home, faded behind them as the convoy pulled into the fog.

The new location was a flattened field outside a bombed village. The land smelled of ash and frozen mud. Shells had stripped the trees bare. Stone walls stood like broken teeth along the ridge.

They had barely set up their tents when the first wave of casualties arrived.

Shouts echoed across the field. Medics scrambled. Nurses ran to triage stations. Clara slipped on her gloves and moved.

A soldier stumbled from the back of a transport, bloody and dazed. Another was carried on a stretcher, unconscious, with half his uniform missing. A third was helped down gently, groaning through clenched teeth.

Clara moved between them, assessing wounds, calling for morphine, checking pulses.

Then a medic appeared at her side. "Evans! There's one more in the truck—unidentified. No tags. Wounded in the leg. Took shrapnel to the side."

Clara ran.

She climbed into the back of the truck, where the dim light illuminated a motionless form sprawled across the floor. His shirt was torn, stained with blood. His face was turned away, half-shadowed by grime and dried sweat.

Her heart stopped.

She knelt beside him. "Sir? Can you hear me?"

No response.

She reached for his pulse—steady, but faint. Her eyes scanned for identifying marks—unit number, initials. Nothing.

But then she saw it.

A faded red thread sewn into the edge of the collar. A small, nearly invisible detail—but one Clara had stitched herself into James's uniform before he left. A quiet secret between them.

Her hands trembled.

"James?" she whispered.

His head stirred slightly. He groaned.

"James, it's me. It's Clara. You're safe. You're home."

His eyes blinked open, unfocused. Then slowly—so slowly—they locked onto hers.

"Clara…" he croaked.

She pressed her hand to his cheek, tears already streaming down her face.

"I found you," she whispered. "I told you I would."

James was rushed to surgery.

The shrapnel hadn't pierced any major organs, but he had lost a lot of blood. Clara wasn't allowed in the tent during the procedure—protocol. So she sat outside, hands clasped, rocking slightly as if in prayer.

The other nurses brought her coffee. Nora placed a hand on her shoulder. Marie whispered, "We were all waiting with you."

When the surgeon finally emerged and gave her the nod, Clara collapsed into Marie's arms.

James woke later that night.

Pale. Weak. But alive.

Clara sat beside his cot, holding his hand in both of hers. She had so many things to say—letters to repeat, stories to share—but in that moment, all she could do was rest her head against his chest and listen to his heartbeat.

"You came," he whispered.

"I never stopped," she said.

He smiled faintly. "You're not just a dream, then."

"No," she whispered. "I'm your home."

Chapter Seven: Chasing Shadows

For the first time in months, Clara allowed herself to exhale.

James was alive.

Bruised. Weak. Covered in stitches and wrapped in gauze—but breathing. Talking. Looking at her like she was the only thing in the world that still made sense.

His cot was positioned at the far end of the recovery tent, near a canvas flap that opened to the field beyond. Clara had moved her writing supplies beside him and took every break she could sitting by his side, reading quietly or just watching his chest rise and fall.

"You haven't changed," he said one afternoon, voice raspy from rest.

Clara smirked. "You're lying. I've got new scars. A dozen new calluses. And a lot less sleep."

He reached for her hand, wincing slightly. "You're still beautiful."

She squeezed his fingers. "You're lucky I found you before the infection did. Another few hours and you might not have made it."

James was quiet a moment. "I would've known if you were close. I would've held on longer."

They didn't say much after that.

Sometimes words weren't necessary.

Sometimes love lived in silence, in the brush of a hand or the sound of shared breath.

Over the following week, James began to heal.

He could sit up on his own by day five. Walk—clumsily—by day eight. The surgeons were impressed with his resilience. Clara wasn't surprised.

"He's stubborn," she told Nora with a grin. "Always has been."

Word spread quickly through the tent about the nurse who found the soldier she loved on the battlefield. Some rolled their eyes. Most whispered about fate. But no one denied the power of it.

Even the surgeon cracked a smile one evening. "Whitaker, you must have nine lives."

James replied, "No, sir. Just one woman who doesn't quit."

But war didn't pause for love.

On the tenth morning, Clara was summoned to the command tent.

Major Leland stood behind a desk cluttered with paperwork and dispatches. He didn't look up as she entered.

"We've received orders," he said flatly. "We're rotating the surgical team north. There's been a breakthrough near Cassino."

Clara's breath hitched. "North?"

"You're on the list, Evans. Departure in forty-eight hours."

Her heart dropped.

"Sir," she said, voice steady despite the storm rising in her chest, "Private Whitaker is still recovering. He won't be moved for at least another week."

"I'm aware."

"Then I'm requesting to stay behind until he's cleared for transport."

Leland finally looked up. "Denied."

Her jaw clenched. "With respect—"

"You're a nurse, not a wife. You go where the wounded are needed. That's your duty."

Clara felt the sting of those words more deeply than she expected.

Duty.

She had followed it across an ocean, into operating tents and midnight triage. She had obeyed every order. Sacrificed sleep. Faced death.

But now, the man she loved—*the reason* she had crossed into war—was here, and she was being told to walk away.

She nodded once, sharply, and turned on her heel.

Clara waited until just before dusk to tell him.

James sat propped up on his cot, his leg wrapped in fresh bandages, a book open in his lap. He wasn't reading—he was watching the sun sink behind the ridge, the light catching in his hair like copper. The quiet surrounded them like fog, thick and waiting.

She knelt beside the cot, resting her arms gently across the edge.

He looked at her and knew.

"What is it?" he asked, voice barely above a whisper.

She tried to smile. "They're rotating us north. Cassino. It's urgent."

James didn't speak right away. He closed the book and set it aside.

"When?"

"Two days."

His jaw tightened. "And you asked to stay."

"I did."

He nodded, swallowing hard. "Let me guess—they said no."

"They reminded me I'm not your wife. Just a nurse."

He turned toward her fully now. "That's a lie."

She blinked, confused.

"You're not *just* anything," he said. "Not to me. Never were."

She reached for his hand. His grip was weaker than it had once been, but still strong enough to make her breath catch.

"I just found you again, James. After everything, I'm not ready to let go."

"You're not letting go," he said. "You're doing what you were called to do. Same as me."

"That doesn't make it easier."

"No," he agreed softly. "But it makes it worth it."

The tent was quiet except for the muffled sounds of distant artillery fire—so far off it could have been thunder.

James leaned back against the pillow and stared at the ceiling. "Promise me something?"

"Anything."

"If we lose track again… if letters stop, if orders get scrambled… you don't wait in fear. You don't stop moving. You *keep going*."

She shook her head, tears starting. "Don't talk like that."

"I have to."

"No."

He looked at her gently. "Clara. You crossed oceans to find me. You've already done the impossible. But the war's not done with us yet."

She pressed her forehead against his. "Then we fight harder."

"I'll keep writing," he whispered. "I'll find you in the next place. Like you found me."

"You better," she breathed.

They kissed—not with desperation, but with something deeper. A sealing of a promise. A vow that didn't need church bells or rings to mean forever.

That night, Clara sat under a blanket just outside the recovery tent, writing by lantern light. She stared at the paper for a long time before her pen began to move.

December 20, 1942

To the future version of us,

If you're reading this, it means we survived.

Maybe we're on the same porch again, or maybe we're in a house we've never seen before. Maybe we're still waiting—but alive.

I want you to know that this was the hardest thing I ever did. Walking away from the one thing I spent months trying to find.

But I did it because you asked me to.

Because love doesn't chain us—it pushes us forward.

I'll see you soon. I believe it.

Always,

Clara

The trucks rolled out before dawn.

Clara didn't look back.

She couldn't. She had already said everything that needed saying. Another glance, another touch, and she wouldn't have had the strength to climb into the truck beside Nora and Marie.

The road to Cassino was a ragged scar across the hills—deep with ruts, soaked with snowmelt, and flanked by the wreckage of burned-out vehicles. Each hour brought them closer to the front. The sky grew darker. The air heavier.

No one spoke much.

Clara sat with her arms wrapped around her medical bag, James's last letter folded inside her coat pocket, her mind playing and replaying every word he had whispered to her.

"Keep going."

She did.

The field hospital near Cassino was worse than anything she had seen. Shelled buildings surrounded the site, and the operating tents were patched with layers of canvas and tarps to block out the cold. The air stank of smoke and antiseptic. Soldiers lay in rows on makeshift beds, shivering under threadbare blankets.

A nurse from another unit met them at the gates.

"Hope you brought strong stomachs," she muttered. "We haven't slept in three days. We lost two surgeons last week."

Clara's chest tightened. But she stepped forward anyway.

"We're here now."

The work was endless.

Shell shock. Gangrene. Amputations. Smoke burns. Clara's hands barely had time to dry between patients. She assisted with surgeries, administered morphine, cleaned wounds until her back gave out. But she never complained.

Every man she treated reminded her of James.

Of what he had endured. Of what he might still be enduring.

Each night, she collapsed onto her cot and whispered his name like a prayer.

James. James. James.

On the sixth day at Cassino, a courier arrived.

He brought three telegrams—one of them addressed to her.

The envelope was wrinkled, damp from snow. Her fingers trembled as she unfolded it.

WHITAKER JAMES L – TRANSFERRED OUT UNIT VIA REDIRECTED FIELD EVAC ROUTE. NEW LOCATION CLASSIFIED. STABLE. REPEAT: STABLE.

She read it twice, then a third time, the words pulsing in her head.

Transferred. Stable. Classified.

Clara stared at the page, her pulse quickening. He had been moved. Again. But he was alive.

She needed more. Needed a name, a base, a village. But the telegram offered none.

Still—he wasn't lost. Not yet.

She folded the note and tucked it with the others in the Bible she kept beneath her pillow.

That night, while snow drifted silently over the broken chapel nearby, Clara sat outside with a candle and wrote him again.

December 27, 1942

James,

They moved you. Again. I don't know where, but I know you're stable. I know you're still in this world. That's enough to keep me breathing.

I'm in Cassino now. It's colder than anything we ever felt in Tennessee. The mountain winds slice right through my coat. But I've seen miracles in these tents. And I'm holding out for one more.

If you're reading this—write me back. Leave a trail. I'll follow it.

I've done it before.

Always,
Clara

Rules had never meant much to Clara when love was on the line.

She had obeyed orders, followed rotations, stitched up strangers. She had played the part of the model nurse. But when she received the telegram about James's transfer—without a destination—something inside her snapped.

She needed more than a telegram.

She needed coordinates.

Three nights after the message arrived, Clara slipped into the administrative tent.

The clerk on duty, Corporal Jenkins, was a lean young man with thick glasses and a nervous habit of tapping his pen. He barely looked up as she entered.

"Need something, ma'am?"

Clara offered him a soft smile. "I was hoping to inquire about a transfer status."

He frowned. "We're not supposed to release personnel movement. Even to medical staff."

"It's not for just anyone," she said. "It's for my fiancé."

It wasn't true—not yet. But in her heart, she had already made the vow.

Jenkins hesitated. "I could get court-martialed for opening sealed movement orders."

Clara leaned forward, voice calm. "All I need is a location. Not a unit number. Not even a name. Just... is he east or west of here? North or south? I need to know he's not slipping through the cracks."

Jenkins looked at her for a long time. Something in her eyes must have landed—the exhaustion, the raw honesty, the desperation sharpened by love.

He sighed, adjusted his glasses, and opened the ledger.

"What's the name again?"

"James Whitaker. 36th Infantry. Last seen near San Pietro."

Jenkins flipped through several pages, his finger scanning lines of dense military script. Clara held her breath.

Finally, he stopped. Tapped once. "He was rerouted to a recovery unit in Atina. South of here. Quiet village. Small field camp. Probably waiting for transport back to Naples."

Clara blinked. "So he's safe?"

Jenkins glanced at her. "Safer than most."

She whispered, "Thank you."

"You didn't get that from me."

"I never saw you," she said, already backing away.

Outside, the stars glimmered above the broken rooftops of Cassino, and Clara stood in the cold with her hands pressed to her chest.

Atina.

One step closer.

She knew better than to abandon her post without orders. But now that she had the name, she could try a different tactic—official channels. A reassignment request. A transport escort. Anything.

She marched straight to Major Leland's tent the next morning.

"I need to speak with you," she said, voice firm.

He looked up from his paperwork. "What now, Evans?"

"I want to request temporary reassignment to the recovery unit in Atina."

Leland raised an eyebrow. "And why would I send one of my best surgical nurses away from a critical zone?"

Clara held out the telegram. "Because someone I love is there. And because I've followed every order you've given me—without hesitation—through snow, bombardment, and blood. And because I can still serve there, just as well as I do here."

Leland stared at her for a long time, then sat back in his chair.

"You went into the records tent, didn't you?"

She didn't answer.

He exhaled slowly. "You could be dismissed for that."

"Then dismiss me," she said, chin high. "But I'm not stopping."

A long pause.

Then—surprisingly—he nodded.

"One week. Temporary assignment. You go. You help. You come back."

Clara's throat tightened. "Thank you."

Leland looked back to his papers. "Don't thank me. Just don't die down there."

The next morning, Clara packed quickly—just the essentials.

She rode to Atina in a supply truck, the road winding through valleys and frost-covered olive groves. When they crested the last hill, the village came into view—a quiet place of stone walls and crooked chimneys, its roads lined with soldiers and weary townspeople.

The recovery camp was tucked behind a crumbling church.

She climbed down from the truck, heart pounding.

The nurse in charge greeted her with a clipboard. "We weren't expecting new staff today."

"I'm just here for a week," Clara said. "But I hear you're short on hands."

The nurse nodded. "Aren't we all?"

She led Clara to the main tent. "We've got twelve beds. Six are post-op. Two are waiting for transfer. And four..."

Clara's voice cut in. "Do you have a James Whitaker?"

The woman paused. "You know him?"

Clara nodded. "He's everything."

The nurse gave her a tired smile. "Second cot from the end. He came in yesterday. Fevered, but holding strong."

Clara's legs nearly gave out.

She walked slowly, past rows of sleeping men, until she reached him.

James lay under a heavy blanket, face turned slightly toward the wall, bandages peeking from beneath his collar.

She knelt beside him, brushing her fingers across his wrist.

His eyes fluttered open.

"You again?" he rasped.

She smiled through tears. "I told you I'd find you."

Chapter Eight: A Reunion in Italy

The days passed slowly in Atina.

Slower than they had in the surgical tents. Slower than they had in the trenches. But for James and Clara, time finally felt like something worth holding onto—something fragile, like breath, like light through dust.

James's fever broke on the third morning. By then, Clara had memorized the rhythm of his pulse, the sound of his cough, the curve of his brow as he slept. She stayed near—quiet, watchful, steady. Not hovering. Just present.

The way he had always been for her.

He stirred often, half-dreaming, half-remembering. Sometimes he mumbled names. Orders. Numbers. But when he opened his eyes, and Clara was there, he always smiled. Even if just barely.

"You look tired," he whispered once.

"So do you," she said. "But we're still here."

He exhaled, the corner of his mouth twitching. "Guess that counts for something."

Once he could sit up, Clara helped him eat—slow spoonfuls of thin broth and soft bread. When the sun warmed the field outside, she helped him to the edge of the tent so he could sit in a chair and watch the smoke rise from nearby chimneys.

They didn't talk much those first few days.

Words felt too heavy.

But sometimes, Clara read aloud—letters he had written her months ago, ones she had folded and unfolded so many times the edges were soft as silk. He listened with closed eyes, his fingers curled gently around hers.

"Did I really say that?" he asked once, when she read a line about how she smelled like summer.

"You did."

He smiled. "War makes poets out of fools."

"Only if they're in love," she replied.

The others in camp gave them space.

Marie winked as she passed by with a tray of gauze. Nora left a sprig of rosemary beside Clara's cot without a word. Even the surgeon, a stiff British major with a cane and a scowl, muttered, "Seems to me he's healing quicker than expected," before moving on.

Clara didn't respond.

But she knew why.

Love wasn't medicine.

But it was something close.

James sat in a folding chair beneath the olive tree near the edge of the camp, his blanket tucked around his shoulders like armor. The winter sun barely warmed the earth, but Clara had insisted he get some air. She stood behind him, massaging the stiffness from his shoulders.

"I missed this," he murmured.

"What?"

"Your hands."

She smiled and pressed her forehead lightly to the top of his head.

They stayed like that for a long time, the only sounds the chirping of birds overhead and the low hum of a supply truck passing in the distance.

"I keep thinking about the ridge," James said suddenly.

Clara froze.

"The one near San Pietro," he continued. "We were pinned down for days. No food. No sleep. Just waiting for the shelling to stop. There was this boy—maybe eighteen. His name was Kenny. From Arkansas. He carried a harmonica. Said it reminded him of home."

James's voice grew distant, a rasp just above a whisper. "The night before the last push, he played it. Soft. Just one song. Something slow. I didn't recognize it, but it sounded like peace."

Clara stepped around and knelt before him, her hand resting on his knee.

"What happened to him?" she asked gently.

James looked away.

"He didn't make it."

A long silence passed between them, full of things they didn't say.

"I still hear that song sometimes," he said finally. "In my dreams. Or when the wind moves through the trees."

Clara took his hand, squeezed it. "Tell me what you need."

He looked down at her, his eyes rimmed red but steady. "I need to know I'm not just surviving."

"You're not," she whispered. "You're living. And you're *loved.*"

She kissed his knuckles, and he leaned down until their foreheads touched, the rough stubble of his jaw brushing her cheek.

"I was afraid you'd changed," he said.

"I have," she replied. "But I still look for you in every room."

"I never stopped looking for you."

That night, back in the warmth of the tent, Clara sat beside his cot as he drifted off. She traced the lines of his hand, now rougher than before, and thought about all the miles they had crossed to find their way back to each other.

And still, fear coiled quietly inside her chest.

Not of death.

But of the next separation.

Of orders. Of distance. Of the war's unrelenting grip.

"James," she whispered, thinking he was asleep.

He stirred. "Hmm?"

"Promise me something."

"Anything."

"If the war pulls us apart again… you won't wait. You'll find your way back to me. No matter how long it takes."

His eyes opened slowly, locking on hers.

"I promise."

Then, almost inaudibly: "Will you marry me?"

The words landed like thunder—and like breath.

Clara blinked, startled. "What?"

"I don't have a ring. I don't have flowers. I'm not even standing up. But I've been carrying it inside me for months. Will you marry me, Clara Evans?"

Tears welled in her eyes.

She kissed him softly, fully.

"Yes," she said. "A hundred times, yes."

There was no white dress.

No aisle, no bouquet, no string quartet playing beneath stained glass windows. But there was sunlight cutting through the cracks in the chapel roof. There was rosemary tucked behind Clara's ear. And there was James, standing in his uniform beside a chaplain with kind eyes and a weathered Bible.

And that was enough.

Word of their engagement spread quickly through the camp. Within days, preparations began—quiet, makeshift, full of the kind of reverence that didn't need polish or tradition.

Nora found a lace handkerchief in her kit and folded it into a veil. Marie gathered wildflowers near the hillside and wrapped them in twine for a bouquet. The cook donated a bottle of wine he'd been saving for Christmas. One of the wounded men—Private Schultz, who had been a jazz pianist before the war—offered to play something on the chapel's battered organ.

Clara barely remembered asking anyone for help.

But help arrived.

Because everyone there—soldier, nurse, or surgeon—understood that love, like life, needed to be celebrated when it bloomed. Especially now.

The morning of the wedding, Clara stood before a cracked mirror in the nurse's quarters, pinning up her hair with trembling fingers.

"You nervous?" Nora asked, adjusting the makeshift veil over Clara's shoulder.

"Yes," Clara whispered. "But not because I'm unsure."

She turned and met her friend's gaze. "It's just… I never imagined we'd get this. A moment like this."

Nora smiled. "None of us did. That's what makes it sacred."

The chapel was just large enough to fit twenty chairs, half of which were filled by patients in robes and slings. The others were nurses, medics, and staff who had carved out time between triage and transport duty to bear witness.

Clara walked down the aisle slowly, her boots brushing against cracked floorboards. James stood at the front, his jacket freshly pressed, a line of stitches still visible beneath his collar.

When he saw her, his breath caught.

"You're the most beautiful thing I've ever seen," he said.

"You need your eyes checked," she whispered back.

The chaplain cleared his throat, smiling at them both.

"War tests the soul," he said softly, his voice carrying through the broken walls. "But love… love is what mends it."

They exchanged vows written on scraps of paper.

James's were short, spoken slowly, each word chosen with care.

"I don't know what tomorrow looks like. But I know it isn't worth anything if you're not in it. I promise to find you—every time. In every storm. In every silence. I'll find you."

Clara's voice trembled, but she never looked away.

"I walked through fire for you. And I would again. I promise to carry your memory, your strength, and your heart—whether you are beside me, ahead of me, or waiting beyond the horizon."

The chaplain paused. "By the power vested in me by a nation at war, and by the love in this room, I pronounce you husband and wife. You may—"

James kissed her before he finished.

And no one minded.

Afterward, the nurses brought out cups of warm cider. Someone lit a candle in an old lantern and set it in the chapel window. Laughter rang through the camp for the first time in weeks.

But it was later, when the crowd had thinned and night had fallen, that the moment truly became theirs.

James and Clara sat on the steps of the chapel, her head resting on his shoulder, his arm around her waist. The stars above them glimmered like ash scattered across the sky.

"We're married," he murmured, almost in disbelief.

Clara nodded. "And somehow, the world didn't fall apart."

He kissed the top of her head. "Not yet."

They had exactly five days of peace.

Five mornings waking to soft light filtering through canvas. Five evenings walking slowly around the perimeter of the field hospital, arms around each other, pretending—just briefly—that the world wasn't burning beyond the hills.

James's color was returning. His limp had improved. The doctor had cleared him for light movement and had even mentioned the possibility of transfer—home, maybe. Or to a stateside base for rehabilitation.

But the war had other plans.

On the sixth morning, a dispatch runner arrived. He handed James a sealed envelope and saluted.

Clara watched from across the field as James opened the orders with shaking hands. She saw the change in his face even before he looked up.

"No," she whispered to herself. "Please, not yet."

He walked to her slowly.

"They're sending me back."

Clara stared at him, willing the words to make sense in some other way. "Back where?"

"The 36th. They're making a push through the valley toward Monte Cassino. They need every man who can still walk."

Clara's lips parted, but no sound came. Her throat was dry. Her hands curled into fists at her sides.

"You're not fully healed."

"I'm functional. And they don't wait for perfect."

Clara blinked fast, trying to hold onto the fragments of the peace they had just begun to build.

"When?"

"Tomorrow at dawn."

A long silence stretched between them.

Then Clara nodded.

"Okay," she said, though everything inside her screamed.

James reached for her hands. "I don't want to go. But I have to."

"I know."

"And I will come back to you."

"You better," she said, trying to smile.

"I'm your husband now," he whispered. "I've got a whole life to show up for."

That night, they didn't sleep.

They lay side by side on his cot, wrapped in one blanket, sharing one breath. James traced lazy circles on her back with his thumb while Clara pressed her ear to his chest, counting the beats like prayers.

"Tell me something to remember," she whispered.

He kissed her temple. "You walked into a war and found me."

"I'll do it again."

"I hope you never have to."

They made love slowly—tenderly—without urgency, as if by drawing closer they could halt the march of time. And afterward, they lay still, listening to the soft sounds of the camp and the wind in the trees.

"I want you to keep the photograph," Clara said, reaching beneath the cot for the worn image of James that had traveled with her across oceans and outposts.

He smiled. "And I want you to keep this."

From his shirt pocket, he pulled a strip of olive drab cloth—his original name tape, torn from a uniform riddled with shrapnel.

She folded it into her palm like scripture.

Dawn came cold and gray.

The trucks were already rumbling by the time James laced up his boots and kissed her one last time beneath the chapel awning.

"I love you, Clara Whitaker."

She cupped his face in her hands. "Then come back to me, James Whitaker."

And then he climbed into the truck.

She didn't cry until it disappeared over the ridge.

Chapter Nine: The Return to Battle

The mountains were sharper than James remembered.

Ridges cut the sky like broken blades. Trees stood like skeletons on the hillsides. The roads twisted through valleys marked with tank tracks and the bones of forgotten vehicles. Everything was gray, cold, and loud.

He had been back with the 36th Infantry for less than a day when the shelling started again.

Monte Cassino loomed ahead.

The Germans held the high ground—a stone abbey fortress that had withstood months of assault. Allied forces were clawing their way up the mountainside inch by inch. Every push felt like dragging the world uphill.

James had barely finished settling into the new command post when the first mission orders came down.

"Advance patrol," the lieutenant barked. "Scouting northeast ridge. Small team. Whitaker, you're leading it."

James nodded, tightened the strap of his helmet, and tried not to think of Clara.

But she was always there.

In the way he scanned the trees.

In the breath he took before moving forward.

In the heartbeat that still echoed steady beneath his ribs.

They moved out before sunrise.

Five men. Cold boots. Mud-caked uniforms. The wind sliced through their coats as they crept through shattered underbrush and the remains of old foxholes. Every step was a risk. Every shadow a warning.

At one point, a mortar shell hit two ridgelines over.

The boom rattled his teeth. One of the younger men dropped to the ground and clutched his helmet like a lifeline.

James knelt beside him. "You're alright. That one wasn't for us."

The kid nodded, eyes wide, hands shaking.

"You got someone waiting for you?" James asked.

"My sister. In Missouri."

"Then hold on. You hear me?"

The boy nodded again.

James stood.

He understood now what Clara meant when she said she wanted to serve to bring men home. It wasn't just about the bandages or the morphine. It was about the *knowing*—the remembering—that every name carried a world behind it.

By the end of the patrol, they had mapped new enemy positions and returned with two wounded. One had taken shrapnel to the shoulder. The other limped badly but stayed quiet.

As James helped them back into the command trench, a captain clapped him on the shoulder.

"Good work, Whitaker."

He barely heard it.

He was already writing in his notebook—Clara's name on the first line. Underneath, he scribbled:

Still here. Still trying.

The first wave came at dusk.

Ambulances rolled into the field hospital outside Cassino like ghosts—headlights dimmed, tires coated in mud. Some carried wounded men barely alive, others held the dead, wrapped in canvas with tags pinned to their chests. The snow hadn't stopped falling since the morning, and now it melted red into the ground.

Clara tightened her apron and ran.

Triage took place beneath a torn canopy. Nurses shouted orders. Medics called for more gauze, more blankets, more morphine. Clara moved on instinct—splinting a shattered wrist, holding pressure to a stomach wound, checking pulses and blinking away tears as she wrote "DO NOT RESUSCITATE" on one man's card.

She didn't have time to think of James.

Until she did.

Until a soldier staggered through the tent flap, bleeding from the temple, clutching his ribs.

And whispered, "Whitaker. Squad leader. He was two rows behind me."

Clara froze.

"Where?" she asked, barely breathing.

The man swayed. "Northeast ridge. Bombardment. We got separated. I don't know if—if he…"

Clara gripped his arm. "Is he alive?"

"I don't know," the man whispered, before collapsing into the arms of a medic.

Clara stood in the chaos, her hands shaking.

She turned toward the row of stretchers still coming in. Her eyes scanned each face—looking for James. Hoping not to find him among the pale, still bodies.

But also hoping, desperately, to find him at all.

Hours passed.

No sign of him.

She stitched a leg, tied off an artery, wrapped a wound so deep she could see bone. Her hands were steady, but her heart felt like it was cracking apart beneath her ribs.

She whispered his name as she worked.

James.

James.

James.

After midnight, Clara stepped into the cold and leaned against the back wall of the hospital tent. Her breath fogged in front of her, and her fingers ached from the cold.

Marie joined her, holding a tin mug of coffee. "You okay?"

"No," Clara said softly. "But I'm still moving."

Marie offered the mug. "That's all we can do."

Clara took it, hands wrapped tight around the heat.

"I think something's happened to him."

Marie didn't offer false hope. Just stood quietly beside her.

"Every time I hear the truck," Clara whispered, "I think I'll see his boots. His coat. That lopsided walk."

"And if you don't?"

"I'll wait for the next one."

Marie exhaled slowly. "You're braver than anyone here."

"No," Clara said. "I'm just in love."

The second push began before sunrise.

James and his squad moved through wet undergrowth, their boots sinking into icy mud. The air reeked of cordite and burned wood. Orders had come down: clear a path northeast of the abbey. Meet resistance. Push through anyway.

By the time they reached the ridge, the shelling had already started.

The world split open in flashes of fire and shrapnel. Men dropped around him—some with cries, some without a sound. James shouted for cover, dove behind a fallen tree, and gritted his teeth against the sting of gravel slicing across his cheek.

"Contact—three o'clock!" someone screamed.

Gunfire erupted from the tree line.

James ducked and returned fire, heart pounding like a drum. His rifle jammed. He cursed and dropped it, reaching for the sidearm at his belt. Before he could draw it, a flash lit up the left side of the ridge—and the world seemed to tilt.

The blast threw him hard.

He landed facedown in the mud, ears ringing, breath gone.

For a moment, there was nothing. Just light. Cold. Silence.

Then—pain.

Sharp, pulsing pain radiated from his side. He reached down, fingers trembling, and felt the warm slick of blood.

He rolled to his back, coughing. The sky above him flickered in shades of gray and flame.

And then, through the fog of pain and fear, Clara's voice.

Not real. Just memory. A whisper pulled from somewhere deep inside him.

"You walk into the fire, I'll follow."

He blinked hard, forcing himself to breathe.

"I'm not done," he muttered aloud. "Not yet."

A medic reached him twenty minutes later.

James was semi-conscious, half-buried beneath mud and torn foliage. He couldn't speak, but he could feel. Rough hands lifted him. Morphine pricked his arm. Someone shouted his name.

He didn't answer.

He was too busy chasing Clara's voice through the haze.

By nightfall, he had been marked for urgent evacuation—tagged and loaded into a transport bound for a nearby triage unit. No one at the hospital yet knew he was coming.

Not even her.

Clara didn't sleep.

She sat outside the surgical tent beneath a patchwork of clouds, her coat pulled tight, hands wrapped around a mug of now-cold tea. The fire in the barrel nearby crackled faintly. Inside, the moans of the wounded rose and fell like a tide. She couldn't look anymore. Not tonight.

She had asked about James three times.

No record. No updates.

Just whispers.

"Whitaker?" one nurse had repeated, scanning the list of incoming names. "Not on the latest transport."

Clara nodded, thanked her, and walked out of the tent before the tears could fall.

Around 5:00 a.m., a Jeep tore across the frost-covered field and skidded to a halt outside triage.

A medic jumped out and waved frantically. "Urgent evac. Multiple wounded. One unconscious—severe blood loss. We couldn't get an ID. No tags. Possible shrapnel to the liver."

Clara stood before anyone else moved.

"Where was he found?"

"East slope. Cassino ridge."

Her legs were moving before she even knew it.

Inside the Jeep, three men were slumped across stretchers. Two were conscious. One was not.

The unconscious soldier's face was caked with dirt and dried blood. His uniform was torn. A pressure bandage wrapped his left side, already soaked through. His dog tags were gone.

But Clara didn't need them.

She knew that jaw. That scar near his temple. That hand— the one she had held while he was fevered in Atina.

She dropped to her knees beside the stretcher.

"James," she whispered, choking on his name. "James, I'm here."

His eyes fluttered beneath bruised lids, but he didn't speak.

A doctor leaned over her shoulder. "We have to move him. Now."

The surgery was brutal.

The shrapnel had missed the artery by less than an inch. Blood loss was critical. Clara scrubbed in. She wasn't supposed to. She didn't care. Her hands were steady. Her heart, a furnace.

For two hours, she assisted—clamping, stitching, suctioning. At one point, James's heart stuttered. The entire room froze.

Clara reached down, touched his shoulder.

"You're not leaving me. Do you hear me?"

He didn't answer.

But the monitor held steady.

He was moved to recovery by noon.

Clara sat beside him, her hair falling from its pins, her uniform stained with his blood. She didn't sleep. She didn't blink.

She just waited.

At sunset, his eyes opened.

Only a little.

But it was enough.

"You again?" he rasped.

She laughed through the tears. "You're a terrible patient, you know that?"

He smiled faintly. "Didn't I promise to come back?"

"You're cutting it close."

His hand found hers under the blanket.

"I remembered the song," he whispered. "The one from the ridge. I could hear it."

Clara leaned in, her forehead touching his.

"You're safe now. You came home."

He blinked slowly. "You were the home."

The nurse on duty approached quietly.

"We'll keep him here for at least a week."

Clara nodded. "He's not going anywhere."

Chapter Ten: Omaha Beach

The letter came folded in quarters, sealed with an unfamiliar wax stamp.

Clara found it pinned to the canvas flap of the recovery tent. No ceremony. No knock on the cot where James lay sleeping. Just a quiet envelope holding the weight of a thousand unsaid things.

She didn't open it right away.

Instead, she sat beside him in the thin winter light, brushing her fingers across his knuckles and listening to his breath—still slow, still steady, but growing stronger every day.

When he finally woke, she was staring at the envelope.

James blinked. "What's that?"

Clara hesitated. "Orders."

He nodded before she could say more. "I figured."

She handed it to him without a word.

He read it slowly. Didn't flinch.

Then he folded the letter neatly and placed it beside his cot.

"When?" Clara asked.

"Four days."

"Where?"

He didn't answer.

But she already knew.

France. The coast. The thing every soldier had whispered about since the year began.

The invasion was coming.

And he would be part of it.

They didn't cry.

They didn't fight.

There was only stillness between them. The kind of stillness that falls between lightning and thunder—when everything holds its breath and waits.

"I can refuse," James said finally. "I could claim incomplete recovery."

Clara shook her head. "You wouldn't."

"I might."

"You won't."

He looked at her then, his eyes filled with more love than pain.

"No," he agreed. "I won't."

Because he knew—like she did—that the war hadn't finished writing its story yet.

And some men were called to carry the ending.

The next few days passed in fragments.

One afternoon, Clara found James packing what little he had into a canvas bag: a spare shirt, a notebook, a worn photograph of her smiling beside a riverbank.

Another night, they walked to the far edge of the camp and stood beneath a sky thick with stars.

"I hate this," Clara whispered.

"I know."

"But I'll never ask you to stay."

"I know that, too."

"You're my husband, James Whitaker."

"And you're my reason."

They didn't kiss. They didn't need to.

They just stood there, fingers laced, letting the cold press around them while their hearts burned too brightly to be dimmed.

The convoy rolled out before the sun rose.

Engines growled. Wheels turned over gravel and frost. Dozens of soldiers stood in the back of trucks, faces hidden beneath helmets and shadows. There were no trumpets, no flags, no speeches. Just a quiet urgency that spoke louder than any farewell ever could.

Clara stood at the edge of the road, wrapped in her long coat, her hands trembling inside her gloves.

James found her in the crowd.

He limped only slightly now, his breath visible in the cold morning air. He looked strong again—tired, but whole.

For a second, they didn't say anything.

Then he took both her hands in his.

"I'll come back," he said.

She nodded. "I believe you."

"If I don't—"

"Don't."

"I need to say it."

She blinked away tears. "Then make it quick."

"If I don't, know that you are the reason I kept going. In mud. In fire. In silence. It was always you."

Her voice broke as she said, "I love you, James Whitaker."

"I love you more."

She reached into her coat pocket and pulled out a small envelope—handwritten, sealed with a pressed blue flower between the pages.

"What is this?" he asked.

"A letter. For when you're afraid. Or alone. Or waiting."

He slipped it into the inside sleeve of his uniform.

"I'll keep it with me," he said. "Always."

Then came the call.

"Load up!"

James leaned in, kissed her forehead. Then her lips. Then her fingertips.

And just like that—he climbed into the back of the truck.

The engine rumbled. The convoy moved.

Clara stood in the road, breath white in the air, until the last vehicle disappeared beyond the hill.

She didn't cry.

Not then.

Instead, she whispered into the wind: "Bring him back to me."

On the boat to Normandy, James sat between two young soldiers playing cards. He stared at the letter inside his sleeve, feeling the weight of Clara's words before he ever read them.

When he finally opened it, the ship rocked gently beneath him.

June 3, 1944

My James,

If you're reading this, it means the sea has already stolen the quiet from around you.

But I need you to know that the only thing louder than war is love.

Mine will be wrapped around you like armor. It will carry you when your strength runs out.

If you close your eyes and listen—you'll hear me.
And if you make it back to me, I'll spend the rest of my life reminding you that you are more than a soldier.

You are my husband.

My home.

My heart.

Always,
Clara

The ramp dropped.

Water surged around James's knees as he waded forward, rifle above his shoulder, boots slipping in sand and seaweed. Bullets ripped the air, cutting down the men beside him before their feet even found land.

The sky thundered. The beach burned.

And still, they ran.

He reached the shore breathless, heart pounding like war drums, his vision narrowed to seconds—duck, shoot, crawl, breathe. The tide pulled bodies backward. Sand clung to the blood on his uniform.

Smoke rolled over the surf like fog.

He couldn't hear his own voice when he shouted orders. Couldn't feel the gash on his arm from flying shrapnel. All that existed was motion and instinct.

But beneath it all—Clara.

Her name pulsed through him like a second heartbeat.

They made it to the seawall.

What was left of his unit took cover behind twisted metal and splintered planks. A boy from Minnesota sobbed into his helmet. Another soldier stared blankly at the ground, rocking slowly, whispering a prayer.

James crouched low, scanning the path ahead. Mortar fire hit the bluff above them, sending dirt raining down.

"We move on my mark," he said.

The others looked at him like he had lost his mind.

"There's no mark to wait for!" someone shouted.

James leaned forward, face streaked with soot and blood. "If we stay here, we die."

And with that—he went first.

The sand was a blur.

He ran low, fast, heart screaming in his chest. Enemy fire lit up the hill. All around him, the world tore apart.

But he kept moving.

He didn't stop until he reached the base of the embankment and turned to fire cover for the men behind him.

Three followed.

Then two more.

Some didn't make it.

But enough did.

And by the time the second wave arrived, James had already marked the safe path with the heel of his boot.

Hours passed.

By dusk, the beach was secure—barely.

James sat slumped against a jagged rock, his rifle across his knees. Blood crusted on his sleeve. His leg ached from a deep bruise. His ears rang.

But he was alive.

Somehow, again—still alive.

He reached into the inside of his jacket, pulled out the letter from Clara, and read it again.

My husband. My home. My heart.

He closed his eyes and whispered aloud:

"I made it."

James didn't seek recognition.

He never had.

But the morning after Omaha, when the commanding officer pinned a bronze star to what was left of his uniform, the other men clapped him on the back, called him a hero, and said things like "damn lucky" and "you saved us out there."

James just nodded.

He thought of Kenny on the ridge.

Of the harmonica song.

Of Clara's letter in his jacket pocket—now stained with sweat and salt and war.

He didn't say much.

But he wrote.

June 8, 1944

Clara,

I made it.

I don't know how to explain what happened. The world exploded and somehow I kept moving. I heard your voice the whole time. You carried me.

They gave me a medal today. But all I could think about was you. I'd trade every ribbon for one more morning beside you, just brushing your hair behind your ear.
I'll write more soon. But I needed you to know—
You were right.

Love is louder than war.

Always,
James

He mailed it that afternoon.

The next morning, a German artillery unit launched a counterstrike near the beachhead—retreating, but not before unleashing chaos along the shoreline. A single mortar shell landed near the medical tent where James was helping load the wounded onto a truck.

He saw it before the others.

And without thinking, he threw himself over the two men closest to the blast.

The concussion knocked the tent sideways.

When the dust cleared, James was alive—but barely.

Shrapnel had torn through his chest.

He never regained consciousness.

The telegram reached the field hospital in Cassino four days later.

Clara had just come off a double shift. Her hands still smelled of antiseptic. Her boots were muddy. When the officer handed her the envelope, her fingers refused to open it.

She already knew.

The weight of it told her.

She walked behind the chapel. Sat on the stone bench where they had spoken their vows.

Then she unfolded the letter James had written days before he died.

She read it once. Then again. Then pressed it to her lips.

She didn't scream.

She didn't cry.

She just whispered, "You kept your promise."

Later that evening, Marie found her there, the letter folded in her lap like a sacred thing.

"He saved two men," she said quietly, her voice steady. "Took the hit so they wouldn't."

Marie knelt beside her. "He was a good man."

"He was the best part of me," Clara whispered. "But I'll carry what he gave me. All of it."

That night, Clara wrote a final letter.

To My James,

You were right.

We didn't need a lifetime.

We needed a story.

And we lived it, didn't we?

You taught me what love looks like when it walks through fire. When it bleeds and prays and keeps going anyway.
You are everywhere. In the quiet. In the wind. In the space between my breaths.

I will go on. I will help others come home. I will keep living—because you did.

And if someday we meet again, somewhere beyond all of this, I'll walk toward you smiling.

And I'll say,

There you are. I've been waiting.

Always,
Clara

Chapter Eleven: The Telegram

The train hissed into Columbia just after noon.

The platform hadn't changed—still lined with cracked planks and iron benches that creaked when you sat too long. The depot clock ticked steadily overhead, indifferent to grief. And the wind smelled like honeysuckle and dust, the way it always had in summer.

Clara stepped down from the railcar with one bag and a folded telegram in her coat pocket.

She hadn't wanted a hero's welcome.

But somehow, word had spread.

Mrs. Jennings from the library stood beside Reverend Caldwell. Clara's father was there too, hat clutched tightly in his hands, eyes rimmed red. Her mother offered no words—just opened her arms and pulled Clara close.

The crowd didn't cheer. They didn't clap.

They just stood silently, hats over hearts, heads bowed.

It was exactly what James would have wanted.

No spectacle.

Just reverence.

The house looked the same.

White porch railings. A cracked walkway James used to hop over as a boy. The swing creaked faintly in the breeze—the one where he first kissed her, long before enlistment letters and battlefield vows.

Inside, the air was still.

Clara moved through the rooms slowly, her fingers brushing the backs of chairs, the edges of picture frames, the dust-covered mantle where James's photo now rested in uniformed stillness.

Beside it sat his Bronze Star.

And the telegram.

She had folded it neatly, pinned it behind the glass.

Because his story wasn't a single moment. It was all of them.

That night, she sat alone on the front porch, wrapped in a quilt that smelled of cedar and memory. Fireflies blinked in the tall grass. The river, somewhere in the distance, whispered against the banks.

She didn't cry.

Not that night.

Instead, she opened the notebook James had carried through the war. The one recovered with his body. Its cover was torn, the spine stitched crudely with field thread.

Inside were names. Coordinates. Brief field reports.

And then, toward the back—

Clara.

Over and over. Her name written in different sizes, sometimes full pages of just that.

And beneath one entry, three words in fading ink:

"You saved me."

The clinic on Garden Street was small—two rooms, a squeaky front door, and a waiting bench that sagged in the middle. But to Clara, it felt like a sanctuary.

She showed up the Monday after returning home, unannounced.

Mrs. Ruth Hammond, the nurse who had run the place since before the war, took one look at her and nodded. "Heard you were back. You looking to sit still or stay useful?"

Clara met her eyes. "I need to stay useful."

"Then grab an apron. First patient's got shrapnel in his shoulder and a mother who won't stop crying."

Clara didn't talk about James at first.

She let her hands speak.

She cleaned wounds, organized cabinets, measured morphine drops with the precision of someone who had counted every second in a triage tent. She didn't flinch at blood. She didn't hesitate with pain.

And slowly, the town came to trust her not just as the girl who lost her husband in France—but as someone who had brought pieces of the war home and somehow managed to keep breathing.

Veterans began showing up.

Boys she'd known as teenagers now sat in her care, thinner, quieter, some with eyes that couldn't hold her gaze.

She gave them space.

But she gave them warmth too.

"Where'd you serve?" one asked as she wrapped his stitched arm.

"Italy. Then Cassino. Then France," she said.

"You see a lot?"

"I saw enough."

He nodded. "You sound like someone who gets it."

"I try."

Her parents were proud, though they rarely said so.

Her mother left breakfast warming every morning before heading to the post office. Her father built a new bookshelf for James's war journals, placing it in Clara's room without a word. It creaked under the weight of folded letters, medals, and notebooks filled with field sketches.

Clara spent evenings reading through them—James's scribbled observations of the land, his notes on troop morale, sketches of hills and helmets and the moon as seen through trenches.

In one margin, she found a tiny drawing of her face.

Beside it: *Still here.*

She traced it with her fingertip, heart breaking and mending all at once.

By the end of that first month home, Clara had fallen into a rhythm.

Clinic in the morning.

Reading in the afternoon.

Letters in the evening.

Always letters.

To widows. To soldiers' mothers. To the men who had survived because James had not.

Each one signed:

"In his honor,
Clara Whitaker"

The invitation came in late July, printed on thick cream paper and hand-delivered by Reverend Caldwell.

Clara nearly turned it down.

"I'm not a speaker," she told him, cradling a tea mug between her hands.

"You're not being asked to speak," he said gently. "You're being asked to remember. For all of us."

The ceremony would be held on the courthouse lawn—an afternoon set aside to honor Columbia's fallen. Twenty-seven names carved into stone, twenty-seven flags planted in the grass.

James's name would be the last read.

Clara hadn't stood in front of a crowd since graduation.

But she said yes.

Not for the attention.

Not for the applause.

For James.

The day was hot and clear.

Families gathered beneath folding tents. Children held paper programs. Veterans wore their dress uniforms and stood with straight backs, the weight of war still stitched into their shoulders.

Clara wore a simple navy dress. Her hair pinned like it had been the day she married him in the ruins of a chapel in Italy.

When Reverend Caldwell called her name, she stepped up to the podium slowly, gripping the folded paper in her hands like a lifeline.

She looked out over the crowd.

And saw not strangers.

But neighbors.

Boys she'd bandaged.

Women who had brought casseroles.

Children whose fathers never came home.

She took a breath.

Then began.

"I want to talk about the quiet things," she said. "Because that's what James was. He wasn't loud. He didn't chase medals. He didn't speak often in crowds. But when he did—when he looked at you—it was with his whole heart."

She paused, blinking against the sun.

"He was a boy who fished in the Duck River. Who carved our initials into the old tree behind Maple Street. He wrote me letters during the war—not to talk about battle, but to ask if the porch swing still creaked. He cared more about people than plans."

Her voice trembled, but didn't break.

"He saved lives. Not just on paper. Not just with orders. He saved people with his presence. With his calm. With the way he made them feel seen, even in the darkest places."

She looked down at the stone markers in the grass, then back at the crowd.

"And now, it's my job—*our* job—to remember those quiet things. To carry their names not just on walls, but in the way we live. The way we show up for each other."

She folded the paper, placed it in her coat pocket.

"And every night when I write to James, I end with the same word. One he gave me."

A long breath.

"*Always.*"

There was no applause.

Just silence.

The kind that meant something had landed.

Then, slowly, people began to stand. Not clapping. Not crying.

Just standing.

And Clara knew she had done what she came to do.

The river hadn't changed.

It still curved through the edge of Columbia like a secret, slow-moving and silver under the late summer sun. Trees leaned over the banks, their branches dipping low. The same flat stones rested in the shallows, worn smooth by time and barefoot splashing.

Clara stood where they'd stood a hundred times before—just past the cottonwood tree, where the grass was patchy and the breeze always a little cooler.

It was where James first kissed her.

Where they'd skipped rocks the week before he enlisted.

Where she once whispered, "I'll find you," and meant it.

She didn't bring a letter this time.

She brought silence.

And she sat in it for a long while.

Birds darted over the water. A frog chirped in the reeds. Somewhere across the field, a tractor hummed toward the end of harvest.

Clara closed her eyes and leaned her head back against the tree.

She tried to imagine James beside her.

Not in uniform.

Not bleeding or broken or brave.

Just barefoot and laughing, his pant legs rolled up, his voice soft.

Just a boy again.

And her—a girl who still believed the world was theirs.

"I'm still here," she whispered.

"And I'm still yours."

Later, she took a pencil and paper from her coat pocket and began to write—not a letter, but an idea. A plan.

A way to turn what they shared into something lasting.

Not a monument.

Not a statue.

Something living.

The Whitaker Fund for Returning Soldiers
Proposal: Create a small clinic in Columbia focused on supporting veterans' mental and physical recovery. Named for James Whitaker, squad leader, Bronze Star recipient, husband, friend.

Staffed by volunteer nurses and therapists.
Funded by local donations and civic grants.
Mission: To give soldiers a place to land. A place to breathe. A place to begin again.

She stopped writing, looked up at the water, and smiled.

The sun dipped low on the horizon as Clara stood.

She brushed the grass from her dress, tucked the paper into her notebook, and turned back toward the town.

She didn't need to say goodbye.

She never had.

Because James had never really left.

He was in every stone.

Every letter.

Every life she helped heal.

Chapter Twelve: His Letters, Her Legacy

Clara waited two months before opening the last letters.

They sat wrapped in a faded red ribbon, tucked inside the back of James's notebook. Four envelopes, each marked with a number in his handwriting. 1, 2, 3, 4. She found them the week after the funeral notice arrived—hidden between sketches and rations lists, as if he'd left them there knowing she'd come looking one day.

She took them to the porch.

The same one where they'd dreamed of Paris, and talked about naming their first child after her grandfather. The swing still creaked. The air still smelled of pine and tobacco.

She opened the first.

Letter 1 – Dated May 30, 1944

My Clara,

If this is the first one you're reading, it means I'm already gone or about to be. I'm sorry for that. I'm sorry I won't be beside you when the world feels too quiet or too loud.
But you need to know—I didn't go into that fight alone. You were there. You've always been with me.

Even before the war, you were my compass. My reason.
If this is all that's left, then let it be a start. Not an end.

Let love build something new.

Always,
James

Her hands trembled.

She held the letter to her chest and didn't move for a long time.

Only after the sun shifted did she open the second.

Letter 2 – Dated May 31, 1944

Clara,

There's a boy in my unit—Thompson. He hums to calm his nerves. The same song, over and over. When I asked him what it was, he said it reminded him of his sister.
That's what I think love does. It gives us something to hold when everything else is shaking.

You gave me that.

So when the wind feels too heavy or the porch too empty, hum something. Let the memory of us fill in the rest.

I'll be there.

Always,
James

Tears slipped down Clara's cheeks.

She didn't wipe them away.

She let them fall.

Because they were his too.

She waited until dusk to open the third letter.

The porch was quiet. Crickets buzzed in the distance. The sky was streaked in lavender and gold. She lit a small lantern and unwrapped the next envelope.

Letter 3 – Dated June 2, 1944

Clara,

If I'm honest, I don't want to be remembered for how I died.
I want to be remembered for how I lived. For how I loved.
I want to be remembered in the smile you give a patient who's scared. In the way you hum when you work. In the way you look at the world like it still has something sacred in it.

Start that clinic. Build that porch swing. Laugh out loud again.

Let me live in those things.

You don't owe grief anything.

You only owe life what we never got to finish.

Always,
James

Clara folded the paper slowly, her hands steady now.

This wasn't goodbye.

This was a map.

And she would follow it.

The fourth letter was the shortest.

She waited until the next morning, sitting at her mother's kitchen table with toast untouched on a plate and the smell of percolated coffee in the air.

The sun streamed in through the lace curtains. It felt like the kind of morning that asked for a beginning.

She opened the last envelope.

Letter 4 – Dated June 5, 1944

My wife,

I saved this one for last because I wanted it to be the thing you carry forward.

No matter what happens, no matter how far the war pulls us apart—

You gave my life meaning.

And I am not afraid.

Tell our story.

Let it matter.

Always,
James

Clara placed all four letters in the wooden box her father had made for James's medals. Then she stood, poured herself a second cup of coffee, and took a sheet of paper from the drawer.

At the top, she wrote in bold pencil:

The Whitaker Clinic for Returning Soldiers
Proposal Meeting – Columbia Town Hall – August 15th

She began listing details—supplies needed, rooms required, volunteer nurses to contact, names of returning veterans she could serve. A second list included James's favorite quotes. One read:

"You only owe life what we never got to finish."

That afternoon, she took the flyer and walked into town.

She posted it outside the courthouse, at the church, and in the front window of the clinic on Garden Street.

And then she waited—not for permission, but for others to feel what she felt:

That love didn't end with loss.

That stories could outlive silence.

And that building something in a man's name was the best way to ensure he was never forgotten.

The Columbia town hall was packed.

Clara stood near the front with her papers neatly clipped, her shoulders straight, her heart thudding like a drum. She hadn't spoken in public since the memorial—but this was different. This wasn't grief. This was building something.

The mayor—Mr. Langford, who'd taught James to fish when they were children—tapped the gavel lightly.

"Miss Whitaker," he said, "you have the floor."

Clara stepped forward.

She didn't read from her notes.

She didn't need to.

"I'm not here to ask for a statue," she began. "I'm not here to raise money for a headstone or a wreath."

She paused. Looked at the rows of familiar faces—shopkeepers, teachers, farmers, and parents of the fallen.

"I'm here to ask for something living. Something that lasts longer than stone or speeches."

She held up a single sheet of paper. "The Whitaker Clinic won't just carry my husband's name. It will carry the mission he lived by: to serve. To protect. To come back home—and help others do the same."

Murmurs swept through the room.

Clara continued.

"There are men returning to Columbia who don't know where to go. Who don't know how to sleep without hearing bombs. Who haven't let themselves cry in years. This clinic will be for them. For their mothers. Their wives. Their children."

A beat of silence.

"James once wrote me, 'You don't owe grief anything. You only owe life what we never got to finish.'"

She lowered the paper.

"I'm here to finish it."

The vote passed unanimously.

By the next morning, volunteers had begun clearing the old post office building near the town square. Planks were removed. Windows washed. Walls scrubbed.

Reverend Caldwell donated pews for waiting benches. Mrs. Hammond brought gauze and antiseptics from the Garden Street clinic. Veterans who hadn't spoken since returning home showed up with hammers, lumber, and—slowly—hope.

Someone painted a wooden sign for the porch:

THE WHITAKER CLINIC – EST. 1944
"Let love build something new."

Clara nailed it in place herself.

One evening, as she stood inside what would become the front exam room, she ran her fingers along the windowsill and whispered, "We're doing it, James."

Outside, the town bell chimed.

The clinic smelled of pine, plaster, and promise.

And for the first time since the war ended, Clara smiled without apology.

The doors opened on a Monday.

There was no ribbon cutting, no brass band, no press. Just the quiet squeak of the door swinging wide and Clara standing behind the front desk, a notebook in her hands and James's photograph framed near the window.

The first to arrive was a boy named Luke Carver.

Twenty-three. Infantry. Returned from France two weeks prior. The town doctor had referred him after he passed out during church and woke up screaming. His mother sat with him on the bench outside, wringing her hands, unsure if he'd walk inside.

He did.

Eventually.

Clara greeted him softly. "Luke?"

He nodded once.

She led him to the back room.

It wasn't much—just a cot, a chair, and a wooden desk with a lamp. But the air was warm. The curtains were open. A pitcher of water sat between them.

Clara sat across from him.

"I don't ask about what you've seen," she said. "Not unless you want me to. You don't have to talk about the war here."

Luke looked down, jaw tight.

"But if you ever want to talk about coming home," she added, "I'll listen."

He didn't speak for a long time.

Then, barely audible: "I see things. When I close my eyes."

Clara nodded.

"And sometimes I think I should've died over there. That maybe the ones who didn't… they were the lucky ones."

Clara's throat tightened. But her voice stayed steady.

"James used to write that the hardest part wasn't the fighting. It was the surviving."

Luke's eyes flicked up.

"James Whitaker," she said. "My husband. He didn't come home. But he sent enough of himself back that I still feel him. In this room. In this place."

Luke swallowed. "This was his idea?"

She smiled. "It was his heart. I'm just the hands."

They talked for an hour.

About nothing and everything.

About home.

About the quiet.

About the nightmares that didn't have names.

Clara didn't rush him.

She just sat, listened, and nodded when he paused.

And when he left, he looked taller—only by a fraction. But it was something.

Over the next weeks, more came.

Some in uniform.

Some barefoot.

Some with anger in their fists.

Others with silence stitched into their skin.

Clara welcomed them all.

She offered coffee, clean linens, and the kind of kindness that expected nothing in return.

She kept James's photograph on the shelf above the supply cabinet.

Sometimes, when the clinic emptied for the day and the light grew long, she'd glance up at him and whisper, "We're doing good, aren't we?"

And in the stillness that followed, she always heard the answer.

Chapter Thirteen: The Return Home

The clinic was quiet.

Sunlight filtered through the tall windows, casting warm lines across the hardwood floors. The smell of coffee and liniment lingered in the air, familiar and comforting. Clara stood in the doorway of the main exam room, her fingers resting on the doorframe, watching as a young nurse bandaged a boy's arm.

She didn't interrupt.

She didn't need to.

They knew what to do now.

It had been almost ten years since she'd opened the doors of the Whitaker Clinic. The building had changed—new paint, new windows, a waiting room with magazines and books—but the soul of it remained untouched.

Healing.

Hope.

James.

Columbia had grown too.

New shops. New roads. More families. But in the middle of it all, the clinic stood like a steady heartbeat. Veterans still came through its doors—some from the Pacific, others from Korea. And now, children of those who'd served came too, bringing their own quiet burdens.

Clara stayed.

She didn't remarry.

She didn't leave.

She lived in the same white house on Maple Street, with the same swing, the same garden, and the same Bible on the nightstand. She kept James's notebook on her desk at the clinic. Sometimes she'd flip it open to the page where he wrote her name over and over again, and just sit with it.

Still here, it read.

And she was.

That spring, she was asked to speak again.

Not at a memorial this time.

At the dedication of a new wing of the local hospital—built in part with funds raised through the Whitaker Fund, which had now expanded across the state.

They called it the James L. Whitaker Center for Veteran Care.

Clara wore navy again.

The same shade she'd worn the day she married him.

She stood at the podium, now older, but still carrying herself with that same quiet strength James had once said he loved her for.

"When the war took him," she said, "I thought it had taken everything."

She paused, glancing at the crowd—young faces, old ones, all listening.

"But then I realized it hadn't taken what mattered most. His heart. His service. His story. Those don't disappear. They multiply—when we let them."

She smiled softly.

"You don't have to serve on a battlefield to be a soldier. Sometimes, you serve by showing up. By standing steady. By helping someone breathe again."

She stepped back from the microphone, and the crowd stood.

Not for applause.

But for memory.

The house on Maple Street was quiet that evening.

Clara stepped through the front door and set her purse down on the table just inside the hall. A vase of fresh daisies sat by the window. The swing out front creaked softly in the breeze, and the kitchen smelled faintly of lemon polish and old paper.

She didn't turn on the radio.

Didn't light the lamp.

The fading orange glow of sunset was enough.

She walked through the familiar rooms slowly—each one touched by time and memory. The photo of James still sat on the mantle, his quiet smile preserved in black and white. A small bronze plaque hung beside it:

"Let love build something new."

She reached for his notebook—the one she had kept in a drawer beside her bed since the war ended. The cover was worn, the spine loose, its pages filled with everything from field maps to fragments of poetry James had never shared aloud.

She turned past the names, the sketches, the plans.

Stopped on the page where her name had been written a dozen times.

Then turned to the very last blank one.

And slowly—deliberately—picked up her pen.

April 1953

James,

I did everything you asked.

I kept going. I kept living. I built something with your name on the front and your heart at the center.

The world is quieter now. Not always kind. But steady.
I see you in the veterans who laugh outside the clinic doors.

I hear you in the clink of my coffee cup against the porch rail.

I feel you in the strength I didn't know I had.

And sometimes—when the night is still—I think I feel your hand in mine.

Thank you for loving me.

Thank you for choosing me.

And thank you for never letting go.

You were my beginning.

And you'll be my forever.

Always,
Clara

She closed the notebook.

Placed it gently back in the drawer.

Then walked out onto the porch, wrapped in James's old army jacket, and sat in the swing that had carried every season of their story.

The sky above Columbia stretched wide and bright.

And in the hush of twilight, she whispered into the wind—just once, and not out of sorrow:

"There you are. I've been waiting."